S/M PASTS

S/M
PASTS

EDITED BY
Cecilia Tan

CIRCLET PRESS
CAMBRIDGE, MA

S/M Pasts

Circlet Press, Inc.
1770 Massachusetts Avenue, #278
Cambridge, MA 02140

Typeset and printed in the United States of America.

ISBN 1-885865-06-6

"Gonar's Saga" originally appeared in *Drummer* 91, as "Bound for Glory."

For more information about Circlet Press Erotic Science Fiction and Fantasy, please send a self-addressed stamped envelope to the address above. Retail, wholesale, and bulk discounts are available direct from us, or through various book distributors including Alamo Square, AK Distributors, Bookazine, Last Gasp of San Francisco, and many others.

CONTENTS

INTRODUCTION

This anthology was born from a series of conversations I had with a friend (another S/M player) regarding our fondness for archaic styles of dress. This particular friend has a penchant for Victoriana, lace, corsets, and the kinds of S/M that fit that milieu: spanking, caning, tea service, and real English-boarding-school stuff. As we talked, we realized there were many other eras of human history, each with their own modes of power exchange, that we and other S/M practitioners evoke with our accoutrements and paraphernalia: ten-gallon hats and spurs, "Gestapo" caps, iron manacles and stocks. Some symbols are modern (such as handcuffs and other current police equipment) or even futuristic (we've noticed a proliferation of Klingons in the leather scene these days), but most of the "hot" images came out of various historical settings: the harem, the dungeons of the Inquisition, the old West and its frontier law, Roman temples ... But, of course, we were aware that it was not a recreation of these settings we were really interested in for S/M play. We did not really want to return to these times (and their ideas of hygiene) but to use our fantasies built on the inherent power exchange in each scenario to create a context for a hot S/M scene.

Or, I thought, a hot S/M *story*. What more perfect way to create the tension of consensual nonconsensuality, than to write stories set in eras where consensuality is a moot point?

This does not mean that all "bottoms" are helpless victims in these stories. One of the things these stories illuminate is that, in S/M fantasy, even when one partner appears to have all the power and the other to have none, a two-way exchange of power still occurs. The balance of power shifts back and forth as each partner plays out his or her role: Inquisitor, temple slave, Prince, army commander, frontier drifter, Bronze Age hero, society debutante, courtesan...

To tell you any more would spoil the tales that await you herein. These authors have served up a smorgasbord of settings, some strictly historical, others slightly fantasy-ized, others complete fantasy with only the bare seeds in the historical past. Devour them.

Cecilia Tan
October 1995

S/M PASTS

Laurie O

THE
INQUISITION

lisabetta awoke, but did not open her eyes; she was
sure that someone was watching her. She could smell
the hay on which she was lying, feel it poking into
her skin through the homespun of her skirt, and it
came to her again where she was: in a holding cell in the
Duke's palazzo, a guest of the visiting Grand Inquisitors. Like
a nightmare, the journey here flooded back into her mind:
being dragged in from the open horse cart in which they had
brought her, manacled, though the trip from her home was
not long; she had burrowed under the hay as much as she
was able, partly to keep warm and partly to keep anyone
from seeing who she was. Thank God they had come during
the day; a torchlit parade at night would have had half the
city out to watch her disgrace. Elisabetta would never forget
the look on her mother's face when the guards had burst in;
somehow someone somewhere in the city had accused
Elisabetta of witchcraft, and she was to be interrogated by
the Grand Inquisitors. And both Elisabetta and her family

knew how few ever returned from a visit with the Inquisition; only one in twenty were found innocent and escaped burning or beheading. Those who returned were seldom the same people who had been taken away, so terrible were the acts performed on them. Elisabetta despaired of ever seeing her family again, or Tonio; nothing in Ferrara had been right since the Inquisitors had come, and she had been stupid to be so careless. Usually only the rich and the powerful were accused, those with lands the Church could seize. There could be few reasons for the daughter of a merchant to interest the Inquisition; either she had been denounced in someone's tortured confession, or Father Federico had made good his threat.

Father Federico had caught her in the woods south of town with Tonio, the miller's son; she and Tonio had been sneaking away there for the past two years, though the priest couldn't know that. Tonio had run off, while Elisabetta froze in fear and shame—only for a moment, but long enough for the priest to reach her and grab her by the shoulders. He delivered a long lecture on the dangers of mortal sin and the pleasures of the flesh—all the while, Elisabetta noted, with her half naked before him, as he did not loosen his grip to let her dress until his sermon was finished. Elisabetta pretended that it was the first time, and cried genuinely repentant tears; her father would kill her if he found out, and she was indeed very, very sorry—that she had gotten caught. Father Federico told her that her only chance to save her mortal soul now was to come to his office the following morning to do some special penance; having only just turned seventeen, Elisabetta was surprised that the penance involved taking off her clothes and submitting to Father Federico. She refused; Father Federico was her own father's age, and how could a man of the cloth expect her to do such a thing with him, especially when he had just denounced it as a mortal sin? You'll do it, he replied, or I'll tell your father about you and Tonio. Go ahead, Elisabetta countered, and

I'll tell him what you tried to do to me. Do that, responded Father Federico, and I'll denounce you as a witch to the Inquisitors who arrived last week. Who do you think they'll believe?

He reached for Elisabetta, and she ducked. He grabbed her hair and pulled her head back, and reached out with the other hand for her cheek; she wrenched free and bit his hand so hard it bled. Her heart was pounding and her only thought was to escape this man who was surely more a servant of the devil than of God. Elisabetta bolted for the door and ran home as fast as she could, heedless of the curses heaped upon her by Father Federico as she fled. She ran to the stable, climbed into the loft, and cried herself out. Hadn't her parents always taught her to obey the priests and do everything the Church required of her? Surely they could not have known about Father Federico ... maybe if she acted as though the whole thing never happened, the storm would blow over. Or so she had prayed, until the palazzo guards came to her family's door.

The iron door grated open, and a silk-clad foot toed Elisabetta's belly.

"Are you awake, then?"

Elisabetta looked up at a tall man, handsome, with a thin black mustache and pointed goatee. He wore the flat, broad-brimmed hat and red robes of an Inquisitor, with ermine trim, ebony buttons, an amber rosary around his neck, and a large mahogany-handled dagger at his waist. It was true what she had heard, then: Inquisitors were wealthy indeed, to sport such costly accouterments.

"You are to come with me, and speak only when you are asked a question."

Elisabetta rose unsteadily to her feet, and the man held forward a brass goblet that he'd been carrying. "Drink this," he said; it was a command and not a question. So Elisabetta drank, holding the vessel awkwardly with her manacled hands. It was a sweet, spiced red wine that may have had more than spices in it; though she had been hoping for water, she was powerfully thirsty and realized she was in no position to make demands or even requests. She was in the belly of the beast, the part of the Catholic Church that sucked men in and swallowed them whole, or chewed them and mangled them beyond all recognition. They would torture her, certainly, until she confessed to whatever they asked, and then they would almost as certainly kill her. She was unalterably in their power, unable to refuse or resist, and Elisabetta suddenly found it difficult to stand.

"Easy," said the man in red, catching her elbow to steady her. He took the goblet back and set it on the ground behind him. "This way." He led Elisabetta out of the cell and down the stone corridor, dark and dank and lit by torches every ten or twelve feet; two of the Duke's palazzo guards followed them.

"I am Ercole. My designation within the Church is not important for you to know, save that I serve Monsignor Gianfrancesco, who will be your interrogator. If you cooperate with us, I will make sure that things go as easily as they can for you." What did that mean? wondered Elisabetta; somehow she did not feel comforted. Presently they reached a large oaken door with iron hinges. Ercole opened it and led Elisabetta inside; the guards took up stations outside the door. Behind a table sat a blond man, bearded and dressed as Ercole was, but even more finely, with a jeweled belt around his waist and a ruby rosary. He stood, and something dark emanated from the man that raised the hairs on the back of Elisabetta's neck. Whereas Ercole seemed quietly determined, Gianfrancesco seemed obsessed; something seethed beneath his surface that he could barely contain. His eyes flitted back and forth in quick, ferret-like movements as he surveyed Elisabetta, studying her from top to bottom. He seemed to stare through her clothes and her flesh itself, probing into her soul; Elisabetta shivered involuntarily. She was afraid, and she knew somehow that this was what he wanted, that the more she feared him, the more delight he would take in making her even more fearful still.

"Elisabetta di Prosperi, you stand before me accused of witchcraft. Do you admit your guilt?" Monsignor Gianfrancesco stood to his full height, which at well over six feet was unusually tall.

"No, sir, I have never practiced witchcraft."

"Father Federico from your very parish says that he saw you in the forest south of here practicing witchcraft."

Magic it might have been with Tonio, thought Elisabetta to herself, but certainly not witchcraft.

Gianfrancesco walked from around the table and stood close in front of Elisabetta; she bowed her head, afraid to meet his gaze. "He showed us a bite-mark on his hand that he claimed had been made by your familiar. Can you explain that?"

Elisabetta paused for a moment; should she tell the truth? Could that get her in any more trouble than she was in right now? "Father Federico ... made advances, and I refused. He tried to ... to grab me, and I bit him."

Behind her Ercole suppressed a smile, and said, with an even voice, "That's not what Father Federico says. He said that he caught you in the forest doing things that would endanger your mortal soul; he feared for your soul, and the souls of your family, and that is why he referred you to us."

"Indeed," Gianfrancesco intoned, placing a finger under Elisabetta's chin and tilting her face up into his; she looked down and away, and their eyes did not meet. "He believed that you were being led astray by others who were enticing you to do the devil's work, and that if you would confess your sins and give us the names of those who were so deceitfully tempting you, you might yet be saved."

A ray of hope cracked Elisabetta's despair. At least Father Federico had not recognized Tonio, and perhaps, if it was thought that she still might be saved, they did not yet plan to kill her.

"Look at me," Gianfrancesco shook Elisabetta's chin and forced her to look at him. "Are you a witch?"

"No," said Elisabetta, with a defiance that surprised even her.

"Have you ever practiced witchcraft?"

"No."

"Has anyone ever enticed you to do the devil's work?"

"No."

Gianfrancesco dropped Elisabetta's chin, abruptly. "I will ask you again in a little while. If you do not change your answers, you will never leave this place."

Ercole led Elisabetta into the center of the room; she felt numb, and it did not occur to her to resist. When he removed her manacles and began to bind her hands together with rope, however, fear shook her again, and she struggled to escape. Instantly Gianfrancesco was behind her, holding her fast while Ercole finished and let the long end of the rope fall to the ground.

"Spread your legs," said Ercole, and Elisabetta noticed for the first time two iron rings set into the floor about three feet apart. Ercole looped rope around her ankles and secured her to the rings, and then tossed the free end of the rope over the open beam above her. He pulled until her arms were stretched above her head, then tied the rope securely to the same ring in the floor to which her right foot was bound. Elisabetta realized that she could not move much in any direction, nor could she fall; should she pass out, the rope from her wrists across the beam would hold her upright. She stood stock still, wondering and fearing what they had planned for her.

Ercole stepped back and looked Elisabetta up and down. "Her clothes?" he asked Gianfrancesco.

"Go ahead," replied Gianfrancesco.

Ercole removed the mahogany dagger from its sheath at his waist and grasped the thick handle firmly. He turned its blade sideways and slipped it between the top of Elisabetta's bodice and her shift; in one smooth, deft move he twisted the blade and cut down and away, opening her dress all the way down to the hem. Elisabetta bit her tongue to keep from crying out. The blade was sharp, and soon Ercole had extended the rent to each side; he stepped behind her and connected each cut up to the neckline, pulling the dress away as soon as the last cut had it free. Then he slit a long U in the back of Elisabetta's shift and pulled the thin muslin away, exposing her naked back and buttocks to the air.

So distracted was Elisabetta by the removal of her clothes that she hardly paid attention to Gianfrancesco as she saw him take the whip down from its place near the door and uncoil it experimentally, out of the corner of her eye. She did not realize what that meant until he cracked it close behind her and she jumped, at least as far as she was able under the circumstances. Ercole took up a position near the door, well out of Gianfrancesco's way, and Gianfrancesco connected his first stroke.

Elisabetta had never been whipped before, and the impact came as a shock. She gasped as the air rushed out of her, and her first thought was that if she hadn't been tied there, she surely would have fallen over. It took several seconds before she felt the sting, and the second blow surprised her as well, coming just as the first was beginning to hurt. It took less time to feel the second blow, and even less to feel the third; by the fourth lash Elisabetta had learned the rhythm of it, and began stretching away from the whip as far as she could—which wasn't very far. It seemed to her at first that the whipping was going to be something she could bear; the first few strokes hurt, but not more than she could handle. Then the fifth stroke hit twice as hard, and Elisabetta began to cry out. The next stroke seemed even harder, and so did the next; soon Elisabetta found it difficult even to scream, as she found that she stopped wanting to breathe. Surely he would stop soon, reasoned some part of her mind, and put the questions to her again? Surely he had to stop...

But thwack! the whip would strike again, drawing a moan or a cry or a scream from Elisabetta, whatever sound she had the strength to make at that moment as she writhed as far away as she could, and the breath caught in her throat. She would freeze then, unable to move, until her lungs of their own accord began to suck the air back in. Then thwack! would come the next blow, relentlessly, and again, until the beads of sweat and blood on her back swelled and trickled together, and Elisabetta spent more time not breathing than breathing, and the world became blissfully black. She slumped in the ropes and Ercole caught her, cutting the long rope with his dagger and lowering her to the floor.

"Two more strokes and she would have confessed, had we not lost her," said Gianfrancesco. "Take care of her, and bring her back tomorrow. I'll be a little more careful next time."

■ ■ ■ ■

Elisabetta lay on her stomach in the straw of her cell, unconscious. Ercole sat with a bowl of herbal salve, the same salve he had mixed for a hundred others in the past, and daubed it carefully on Elisabetta's back. It would help the gashes heal cleanly without becoming infected, and would take some of the pain away. Once a subject had passed out, there was no point to ill treatment; the subject couldn't feel it, and it would not advance your goals. Better to care for them well, build their strength back up, prepare them for another round. He propped Elisabetta into a sitting position, her side against the wall; she would not come fully awake. Carefully he spooned porridge into her mouth; reflexively, she swallowed it, and Ercole watched her closely. It took a long time to empty the bowl, but any faster and Ercole feared she might choke. He sighed. Elisabetta would be his last subject, and he wanted to be perfect for her.

It was not the physicality of what the Inquisition did that disturbed Ercole. Having gone through many deprivations and tortures himself, he knew that they brought you to a place that a thousand Hail Marys never could. No one experienced spirituality more clearly than when in suffering; it purified the soul, leaving the mind clean and blank in a way that nothing else could. It was more the corruption that bothered him, the trading of bodies for riches, and the fear of the victims when they arrived. They could not know how ecstatic, how purifying their experience was going to be, and he could not tell them. That, and the fact that so many of their victims were killed, regardless of their guilt or innocence, simply so that the Church or some greedy lord could take possession of their lands. Ercole didn't care that it was for the good of the Church; he was always letting people go. After a dozen chastisements, the Cardinal finally decided to let him leave the Inquisition and minister his own parish. After he completed one more assignment—this one—he would be free. And if she were strong and clever enough to please Gianfrancesco, so would be Elisabetta.

■ ■ ■ ■

Elisabetta woke to daylight, realized that she was now completely naked and hungry, too, and wondered how long it had been since she had last eaten. Had she slept for hours or days? The wine could have contained a sleeping potion, and it was impossible for her to tell. Her back ached dully but no longer burned; did that say anything about how long she had slept?

The cell door opened and Ercole entered; dimly Elisabetta noticed that he didn't bother to manacle her this time. He helped her stand, gently, but saying nothing, ignoring her nakedness. Again he offered her a goblet of the sweet spiced wine; again she drained it. He led her down the hall, this time to a different room, and Elisabetta walked with her head bowed.

The room was large, with a cavernous ceiling. A long, sturdy table stood in the middle of the room, with a strangely shaped piece of iron hanging above it, suspended by chains from the ceiling. Coils of rope hung from hooks on the wall to the right. Along the far wall a fire blazed in a broad fireplace; several copper pots full of some sort of liquid sat on the hearth at the edge of the fire, glowing hot. Next to the fireplace sat a small table covered with earthenware bowls, fat tallow candles, and a few odd objects made of tin, copper, and brass. A well was set into the floor at the left corner of the room, a winch and rope above it and a small bucket resting to one side. All this Elisabetta took in with a glance; she was not sure that she would ever leave this room again, and every detail impressed itself into her memory.

"How lovely to see you," said Gianfrancesco drily, stepping in front of her again. "Have you any answers for me today?" He reached for Elisabetta's chin and forced her to look at him again. "Are you a witch?"

"No," said Elisabetta softly. What could she say but no? If she said yes, they would surely burn her at the stake, and she couldn't imagine anything they could do to her that would be worse than being burned alive.

"Have you ever practiced witchcraft?"

"No."

"Has anyone ever enticed you to do the devil's work?"

"No," whispered Elisabetta, fearing what this answer would bring but unable yet to betray Tonio or anyone else to these horrible men.

"Then we will start afresh today. Ercole, take her to the table."

Ercole led Elisabetta to the long table in the center of the room and bent her over it; Gianfrancesco took a short length of rope and bound her hands together behind her back, leaving several inches of rope loose between them so that her hands did not touch but could fall apart no farther than the width of her hips. They pulled Elisabetta onto the table then, on her stomach, and Gianfrancesco winched down the iron rack above her to a height level with his head. Ercole wound rope around each of Elisabetta's legs and ankles, tying them separately to the apparatus above, stretching the ropes just exactly the length they needed to be without sagging or pulling Elisabetta off the table.

Meanwhile Gianfrancesco slipped rope beneath Elisabetta's hips and ran three more loops around her body, encircling her at the waist and just above and below her breasts. Then he fastened a rope lengthwise along Elisabetta's torso, weaving it over and under the loops already there; Ercole followed Gianfrancesco, mirroring his weavings on the right. Ropes were attached to the four knots now at Elisabetta's hips and shoulders, and these were tied to the rack overhead as her legs had been. Then Ercole attached the rope between Elisabetta's hands to the rack, not pulling it high enough so as to cause her pain, but high enough so that her hands could not touch her back. Elisabetta sank down farther inside herself, more aware with each turn of the rope how helpless she was, and now constantly aware that she did not have the use of her hands.

Gianfrancesco stepped over to the wall and turned the winch attached to the iron rack from which Elisabetta hung. He raised the rack until Elisabetta was several inches above the table and her head hung down. Ercole slipped a leather headpiece under Elisabetta's forehead; it fit like a hatband, buckling around the back of her head, with two long straps attached at either side. The length of the straps adjusted with buckles, and the straps ended in hooks. Ercole fitted the hooks securely into the holes in the rack designed for them, and adjusted their length until Elisabetta's head was in line with the rest of her body. He gave her an experimental push on the shoulder, and she swung freely; he nodded to Gianfrancesco, who gave the winch an additional turn. Then

Ercole dragged the table out from under Elisabetta and over to the wall by the door, and Elisabetta hung suspended in empty space, swinging very slightly from side to side.

Elisabetta was terrified. All she could see was the small patch of stone floor beneath her, though she could hear every sound that Ercole and Gianfrancesco made, and found herself straining more and more to try to hear every single thing that they did, so that she might have some clue as to what would happen next. She was terrified that she might fall at any moment, and even more terrified at what they might do to her now that she was tied in such a helpless and vulnerable position. She had never imagined that she would be trussed up and hung like a deer carried home from the hunt, and though the ropes were not actually causing her any real discomfort yet, they seemed to burn her skin. Her heart pounded, and she did not know whether to wish that they would begin soon, so that she wouldn't have to wonder any more, or wish that they would delay, so that she wouldn't have to face the things they would do to her for at least a while longer.

Suddenly Gianfrancesco was right in front of her; she could hear his breathing, and see his feet. "Ercole, your dagger." Gianfrancesco took a step away; Elisabetta could hear Ercole drawing the dagger and the rustle of Gianfrancesco's robes as he must be taking the dagger and carrying it over to the table by the fire. She heard the faint slosh of liquid in a bowl and droplets hitting the table as though something had been shook, and then Gianfrancesco was back in front of her again. He went down on one knee and tilted her head up by the chin so that she could see his face.

"Do you see this, Elisabetta?" Gianfrancesco held up the dagger, holding it at the balance point between the blade and the handle. The handle gleamed wetly and smelled of olive oil; it seemed immense so close in front of Elisabetta's eyes now, and she remembered how large it had looked to her even from across the room when she had seen Ercole wearing it. "I promise, as long as you hold this inside you, I won't cut you with this or kill you with it." He walked around behind Elisabetta and between her legs; she squeezed her eyes shut as she felt first the blunt butt, and then the entire length of the dagger handle pushed inside her up to the hilt. It felt wide, very wide, and her outer lips contracted reflexively; she felt stuffed so full she could hardly breathe, and she couldn't imagine it falling out.

"The sharpest edge is down," said Gianfrancesco. "Try not to move too much, or you may turn it around and cut yourself." He walked around in front of Elisabetta again, not bothering to kneel this time. Elisabetta could hear Ercole walking over to the table and picking something up, and then joining Gianfrancesco in front of her.

"We will start with question one. Are you a witch, Elisabetta?" Gianfrancesco intoned.

"No," said Elisabetta. She saw the flash of light out of the corner of her eye just before she felt the candle-flame brush across her left nipple; she gasped as it continued across her right. Just as she was thinking that it had hurt, but not as much as she would have thought, she felt the sharp sensation of hot wax dripped on her right shoulder. "Oh...," she cried out in surprise and pain. Before the pain from these first few drops faded, a line of hot droplets peppered across to her left shoulder, and after the briefest pause, another line splattered below it across from left to right. It burned, and Elisabetta moaned.

"Are you a witch, Elisabetta?" It was Ercole's voice this time, softer, almost intimate. She could hear Gianfrancesco walking to the table and coming back again; no doubt he had candles, now, too.

"No," she repeated softly, and gasped as she felt hot wax trickling down over the soles of her feet.

"All you have to do is say yes, and we can stop." said Ercole, moving to Elisabetta's right side. He held the candle horizontally above Elisabetta's back, skillfully guiding the drops of melting wax between the welts from the whipping, where they would roll to the edges of the salved gashes and itch once they'd dried. "Just one simple word, very easy, and you can stop all this from happening. Are you a witch?"

Elisabetta said nothing but moaned; the nerves on her back were aflame, and the wax that fell between her welts seemed four times hotter than it actually was. At the same time Gianfrancesco had begun to drip wax randomly across the backs of her thighs and buttocks; she could not predict where or when the next drop would fall, nor could she shut out the angry bees that stung her back. She squirmed in the ropes, feeling the dagger hard inside her, stretching the walls of her vagina wide apart, and feeling each place that the rope crossed and tugged at her skin. She closed her eyes and felt for an instant suspended ten feet above her own body; she had the eerie sense of drifting back and forth between her body and this space above it for several long moments, and then dropped mercilessly back down into her body, back into the ropes and heat and wax.

"Strain as hard as you like. You can't go anywhere, and you are running out of time." From somewhere far away Elisabetta heard Gianfrancesco's voice, heard him walk to the fireplace and pick something up from the hearth.

Then Ercole was in front of her again. "Elisabetta, have you ever practiced witchcraft? Come on," he said, in a seductive tone, close in front of her face. "I need an answer."

Suddenly something searing hot poured down the back of Elisabetta's ass cheeks and down the backs of her thighs; Gianfrancesco was pouring spoonfuls of hot wax onto her. She cried out, but he continued in a slow, steady, methodical rhythm. Elisabetta struggled in the ropes, but as Gianfrancesco had pointed out, she had no where to go.

"Elisabetta," Ercole whispered in her face. "Do you want us to stop? Do you? Have you ever practiced witchcraft?"

"Y—no," moaned Elisabetta, almost a sob, as she caught herself just in time.

"No? No? You don't want us to stop? Well, I wouldn't want to disappoint you." Ercole withdrew and Elisabetta could hear him over by the fireplace. Gianfrancesco stepped around in front of her, and Ercole handed him something.

Suddenly beneath her Elisabetta saw two large earthenware bowls, filled to the brim with hot wax; Gianfrancesco set them on the ground. Slowly Ercole began winching her down, and Elisabetta realized what was going to happen. Her breasts, which had been hanging down for quite some time and were completely engorged with blood, were very sensitive. Elisabetta could feel the heat rising from the wax more and more intensely the closer she got to it, and her breathing grew shallow. Ercole stopped just a heartbeat above the surface, where one deep breath on Elisabetta's part would dip her nipples into the wax. Elisabetta trembled. She knew that if she said something, if she said yes as Ercole had asked, they would stop, but she could not bring herself to do it. She heard Ercole turning the crank again, but for some reason, she was staying where she was and not moving any lower; she could not see that Ercole had engaged the brake and was about to release it.

Before Elisabetta could think or even breathe she dropped the final few inches, and her breasts were completely submerged in the bowls of hot wax. She screamed once as all the air rushed out of her; an infinite amount of time later Elisabetta breathed in again, and Ercole slowly raised her back up again into the air. The wax began to cool and harden, and Elisabetta felt it shrink and squeeze her breasts.

Ercole came back from the wall and picked up a short length of rope. He tied it tightly around the base of Elisabetta's breasts as they hung down, while Gianfrancesco held a short stick to the outsides of her breasts to be included in the knot at the outside of the loops. Gianfrancesco grasped the stick at Elisabetta's left breast and gave it a half-turn; Elisabetta gasped, as she had thought the rope to be tight before. Ercole worked at Elisabetta's right breast, tightening that loop by a half-turn as well.

"Are you a witch, Elisabetta?" Gianfrancesco tightened his side by another half turn. "You know the answer I want to hear."

"Have you ever practiced witchcraft?" Ercole gave her right breast another half-turn. "Say yes and you can stop the pain."

Elisabetta's head swam; her breasts felt like they would explode, and she wanted desperately for the pain to stop, but she knew she could not answer yes. So she said nothing, but hung in the ropes and breathed.

Ercole and Gianfrancesco tied the sticks down where they were, and left Elisabetta's breasts to hang and throb on their own. She could feel the cooled wax on her skin crinkle and itch as she fruitlessly tried to shift into a position that would lessen the throbbing. Ercole walked around behind Elisabetta and she could feel him pull her ass cheeks apart, careful of the dagger, and gently run a finger around her anus.

"I would say she's a three," he called to Gianfrancesco, who had moved to the table by the fireplace.

"Then we'll use a five," replied Gianfrancesco. Elisabetta craned her head to see what Gianfrancesco had picked up, and caught a glimpse of what looked like a long, strangely curved metal funnel, with a closed bulb like a radish at the narrow end. Gianfrancesco dipped the funnel in olive oil and brought it over to Ercole. Ercole brought it to Elisabetta's ass, pointed-radish-end first, and gave an experimental push.

"It's too big," he said. "It won't go in."

"Than use heated oil," replied Gianfrancesco impatiently. "That is the one we are going to use, one way or another."

Ercole did not sigh, though he wanted to, but merely walked over to the hearth, wrapped his hands in the loose folds of his robe, and got the bowl of olive oil that had been heating by the fire. He came back to Elisabetta, set the bowl down, and put the funnel in the oil so that the cold metal would grow warm. He dipped his fingers in the oil, and slipped his left index finger into Elisabetta's anus. She tightened up at first, but began to relax as Ercole dribbled on more oil and massaged her. Still, he could only fit one finger in. Experimentally he reached down between Elisabetta's legs with his right hand, first turning the sharp edge of the dagger to the left, and found the pearl of her clitoris. Ercole glanced to see what Gianfrancesco was doing; he had gone over to the well in the corner to draw a pail of cold water. Good; that should give him a little time. He began to massage with both hands, and could feel Elisabetta's surprise. She hadn't expected a sensation like this, but she was just as powerless to resist it as she had been all the other sensations she'd been through. And she was probably also surprised, Ercole thought to himself, at how aroused she already was. She was new to the experience, and did not yet know how tissue-thin the boundary could be between the ecstasy of sex and the ecstasy of torture. He could feel her dissolve, and soon he could slip two and then three fingers inside her. Moisture began to ooze out around the hilt of the dagger, and Ercole guessed that it no longer fit as tightly inside Elisabetta as it had before. He withdrew his fingers from her ass and picked up the funnel, still working expertly with his right hand. He pressed the slippery, warm tip of the funnel against Elisabetta's anus, and this time, as he could feel her coming, he pushed and twisted and was able to slide it all the way in. It hadn't taken more than two or three minutes, Ercole thought to himself, and since Elisabetta had had sense enough not to make any noise, Ercole was sure that Gianfrancesco was unaware of what had happened. Gianfrancesco came back then with the bucket of water, and a ladle, and Ercole stepped away to give him room.

To Elisabetta, the whole thing seemed to take much longer, almost an infinite amount of time. And when Gianfrancesco filled the funnel with cold water and she felt the cold rushing deep inside her, she came again from the strangeness of it, though Gianfrancesco no doubt misinterpreted her moans and shudders. After another minute or so, when Gianfrancesco felt that the water was likely no longer cold enough, he swung Elisabetta forward, catching the rope under her hips and swinging her up so that the opening of the funnel pointed down and the water drained back out into the bucket that Ercole held to catch it. Elisabetta gasped as Gianfrancesco swung her up, her muscles contracting in alarm as though she could grab on to something to stop herself from falling back down, then realized how futile this impulse was, as the only thing on which she could clench was the dagger inside her. Gianfrancesco let go and stepped back, and Elisabetta swung dizzily back down, feeling the ropes around her body bite into her as she swung back and forth, a little less far each time until she hung still once more. Her tightly bound breasts, which she had stopped feeling for awhile, began to throb painfully again.

Gianfrancesco nodded to Ercole, who wrapped his robes around his hands again and retrieved a bowl of molten wax from the hearth, returning to his station behind Elisabetta. Gianfrancesco stood in front of Elisabetta, and placed one hand on each outer knot of the ropes tied around her breasts. He toyed with the sticks there as if he would tighten them another turn.

"I'll give you another chance to save yourself some pain," he breathed in Elisabetta's face. "Are you a witch?"

Elisabetta did not answer.

"Have you ever practiced witchcraft?" Gianfrancesco waited.

Again Elisabetta did not answer.

"Very well then. Ercole, proceed." As Ercole began to pour the hot wax into the funnel in Elisabetta's ass, Gianfrancesco pulled on the critical loop and released both of Elisabetta's breasts at once. The sticks spun as they unwound themselves, and the loosened ropes dropped to the floor. Pain exploded outward from both breasts as the blood rushed back into them; it would have been overwhelming, had it not been for the fact the sensations from the hot wax flowing into Elisabetta's anus were overwhelming, too. The metal flange at the outer lip of the funnel carried a lot of the melted wax's heat away, as did the fact that Ercole was pouring it from as high above the funnel as he could, giving it time to cool to the point that would not actually damage Elisabetta when it flowed inside and filled the funnel. But after the cold water from the well, the wax felt blisteringly hot to Elisabetta. She could not decide which she felt more intensely, the hot wax inside her or the pain of her breasts being released; indeed, she was beyond all decisions, beyond thinking, beyond speech. She bucked and writhed, and completely beyond her notice or control, the dagger fell out from between her legs and clattered to the floor. After a short time the pain in Elisabetta's breasts subsided, and she had only the burning heat from the funnel inside her to focus on; suddenly it was removed, and Elisabetta felt weak and empty, hanging light-headed in the ropes, quite unable to move even if she hadn't been so securely tied. She forgot that she had arms and legs; she forgot that she was a creature who could move. Suddenly she was just the essence of Elisabetta, and barely that, floating several feet off the floor, and it barely seemed to matter what might happen to her body.

Gianfrancesco picked up the dagger and wiped it off. "So, my dear, here we are at last. Remember my promise? I must return to Rome tomorrow, and I must confess that I don't have any more time to spend on torturing you. So I'm afraid we must end this rather quickly." He laid the cold flat of the blade against Elisabetta's right nipple; she did not even flinch. "But there is one question that I must have an answer to before we can finish." Gianfrancesco flipped the blade over and pressed the other side to Elisabetta's left nipple; again she did not move. He moved it then to her face, pressing it flat to her left cheek. Some part of Elisabetta felt that she ought to be afraid of the dagger, of what it could do to her, while to another part the dagger seemed like a threat of no consequence. It would only happen to her body, so terribly far away; it was only to her body that Gianfrancesco was speaking, down in the room below her.

"You would not be here if someone had not enticed you to disobey," he continued, slowly bringing the blade away from her face. "And I know that there was someone other than Father Federico who led you to be in the woods where he found you." Gianfrancesco began trailing the point down Elisabetta's back so she could feel how sharp it was, raking through the crusted whip-marks and the patches of wax, pricking the warm, reddened skin beneath.

"There are several ways we can end this, depending on how you answer me. One way, if you refuse to answer, would be to start carving. A 666 right here, for example," Gianfrancesco said, laying a hand on her left ass cheek and drawing the dagger lightly back and forth across it. "I could cut it in deeply and smear it with ash. We could keep you here until it healed over, and then take you out into the market square and show the entire city how you bear the devil's marks. They will burn you right there on the spot. And you know St. Peter would never let you into heaven with the mark of the devil on your flesh." Gianfrancesco drew the knife across Elisabetta's hip and down to her stomach. "Or perhaps a pentagram on your belly would do just as nicely. Or maybe I should cut the sixes"—he brought the dagger straight up from Elisabetta's navel with a feather-light touch—"into your breasts. Everyone in the city will want to examine you closely before they pass judgement. Perhaps they will keep you in the stocks a day or two before they burn you."

Elisabetta did not move. Gianfrancesco put a hand around the top of her left breast and pressed the point of the dagger into the underside; a bead of blood appeared. He moved an inch to the left and raised another bead, than another to the right of the first. The three beads swelled and ran down Elisabetta's breast towards the nipple. Gianfrancesco waited until they collected together there, caught the large droplet on his finger, and smeared it across Elisabetta's lips. She licked them reflexively; they tasted salty, and slightly metallic.

"Your blood, Elisabetta," Gianfrancesco said in a low voice.

The pain reached Elisabetta then; something was hurting, and it was hurting her. With a snap she was suddenly back in her body again.

"Stop. Please."

"Are you with me now, Elisabetta?" Gianfrancesco pulled her head up by the hair and looked into her eyes. "I said that that was one way we might end this. Those could be the starting points for sixes that I carve into you, before abandoning you to the market square. Then again we might also let you go, if you will tell us who enticed you into devilry in the forest." He released her head back into the strap. "Or kill you here and now if you don't."

Ercole, who had been standing silently against the wall, came over and knelt in front of Elisabetta. "Give us a name, Elisabetta," he said, gently but firmly. "You know we'd really like to let you live, I'd like to let you live, but we can't do that unless you help us. Tell us who led you astray."

"Tell us, Elisabetta." Gianfrancesco bent over and raised the dagger to Elisabetta's throat. "Who enticed you? Who? This," said Gianfrancesco, turning the dagger ever so slightly so that the edge of the blade pressed into Elisabetta's skin and a ruby thread of blood welled up, "is the last time I will ask."

The next instant seemed to last weeks to Elisabetta; she knew now with all her being that she wanted to survive, and if giving a name would keep her alive, then she would most certainly give a name. Yet she could not betray Tonio; he was no practitioner of witchcraft, and she could see no reason why the Inquisition should be interested in him.

"If I tell you, you will not kill me?"

"No," said Gianfrancesco levelly, almost reluctantly. "I promised a favor to an old friend." He glanced at Ercole, who returned his gaze unblinkingly.

Elisabetta opened her mouth to speak, not knowing what she would say, and suddenly the name 'Teodora" came to her lips. Teodora was the alderman's wife; if someone had to be sacrificed, it would be hard to think of someone who deserved it more. She was a wicked woman, a gossip, who had the heart and the ear of the Duke. If she took a dislike to you, that was the end of it; she could get the Church to excommunicate you or the Duke to close up your shop. It had happened to Elisabetta's Uncle Salvatore. Teodora had been accustomed to getting the best of everything for free; every merchant in town gave her whatever she admired in their shops, because they feared the consequences if they displeased her. Elisabetta knew of at least one poor baker who had been bled almost dry when Teodora took a liking to his expensive cordial-soaked fruitcakes.

Gianfrancesco increased the pressure at Elisabetta's throat ever so slightly.

"Teodora," breathed Elisabetta. "Please, don't..."

"Teodora? Who is Teodora?" Gianfrancesco lowered the dagger from Elisabetta's throat.

"The alderman's wife. She said she would kill me if I told anyone. She bewitched me and made me go into the forest; she casts spells on those she doesn't like. She cast a spell on my Uncle Salvatore last year; that's why he lost his shop."

Suddenly the dagger was back at Elisabetta's throat. "Do you swear on your mortal soul and the soul of your mother that you are telling the truth?"

"Yes!" cried Elisabetta, surprised at the conviction in her voice. It was so easy, somehow; lying was no more wicked than any of the things they had done to her.

Gianfrancesco dropped the dagger and handed it back to Ercole, commanding him with a look. "I have my own test for how truthful you are being..."

Ercole stepped behind Elisabetta and unbuttoned the front of his robes. Elisabetta felt something warm and hard slip in between her legs; it took her a minute before she realized that it was Ercole. She had no resistance to offer, mental or physical, nor would she have wanted to offer any if she could. She could not move in the ropes, and she was still the vessel for the sensations with which they chose to fill her. Ercole moved and thrust inside Elisabetta, guiding her hips with a hand on either side; Gianfrancesco waited until her breathing grew heavy and ragged.

"Who enticed you, Elisabetta?"

"Teodora," she managed to gasp.

"Who?"

"Teodora! Teodora!"

"It's not too late for me to kill you if you are lying."

"It is the truth, sir!" cried Elisabetta. "You must believe me!"

In response Gianfrancesco reached up to the buckles on the straps that held Elisabetta's head. At first she thought he was going to free her, but instead he tightened the straps so that they pulled her head up, face forward. He unbuttoned his own robes, forced open Elisabetta's mouth, and filled it; she had been hanging at just the right height. He swung her back and forth between Ercole and himself, pulling her to his own rhythm rather than Ercole's. Ercole reached above Elisabetta and steadied himself on the ropes running up from her hips. Elisabetta did not know how she would judge the size of Gianfrancesco's organ under other circumstances, but right now, as it forced her lips apart, filled her mouth with its thickness and beat against the back of her throat, it was much too large. As the head plunged down into her throat it blocked her airway, and the angle was such that the part of the shaft that followed did the same. Only in the brief instant after Gianfrancesco's out-stroke, before he slammed back into her again, could Elisabetta breathe, and then only on the strokes that he came far enough out for her to do so. From what seemed like a long distance away Elisabetta heard Ercole moan as his tempo increased before climax; the sensation of his vigorous thrusts as he came was so intense that Elisabetta came with him, though through no conscious participation on her part. Relentlessly Gianfrancesco kept filling her throat. As he got closer and closer to release, he spent more time deep inside, and the chances for air came fewer and farther between. She tried to relax, tried to tell herself that it was no worse than the wax or the whipping had been, but she could not keep herself from struggling and pulling on the ropes as she fought to somehow push back away from Gianfrancesco far enough to breathe. Finally it became too long between breaths for Elisabetta, and as Gianfrancesco came, she passed out and went limp in the ropes.

Both men withdrew slowly. Panting, Ercole walked over to the table he had earlier pushed to the wall, and began to drag it back underneath Elisabetta. Gianfrancesco stood still with his eyes closed for a moment, breathing, and buttoned his robes back up. He watched as Ercole lowered Elisabetta back onto the table with the winch and began to untie her.

"Do you think she was telling the truth?" he asked Ercole.

"It doesn't matter, does it? She has nothing that you want."

"At least not anymore," Gianfrancesco smiled to himself. "You are right. I'll leave her in your capable hands and check in with you later; I have affairs to attend to to prepare for my journey." He left to go, then paused in the doorway and studied Ercole for a moment. "Enjoy your farewell gift," he said simply, and turned and walked down the dark hallway.

■ ■ ■ ■

It was night when Elisabetta came to herself again. She rolled onto her side, and looked up to see Ercole standing outside of her cell, watching her. "Are you going to kill me now?" she asked softly, "or let me go?"

"I'm going to take you home. Gianfrancesco was telling the truth." Ercole swung open the door to the cell, which had been unlocked. He handed Elisabetta some clothes, an old set of novice's robes, and waited while she put them on. "You have been found innocent and may return to your family."

"And Teodora?"

"Gianfrancesco may take her with him back to Rome, if he decides to question her. He will interview her late tonight after the guards have brought her here. And Father Federico will be accompanying him to Rome; it appears his piety has been in question of late."

Elisabetta paused a moment as she finished dressing. "And you?"

"I am replacing Father Federico. I have been needing a change of scenery. Come; there is a coach waiting outside."

Ercole led the way through the maze of corridors towards the palazzo gate, and Elisabetta followed him, still not quite able to believe that she was free. She wondered silently, as she followed Ercole, just how far Gianfrancesco's favor extended, and whether Ercole's staying here was part of it. Perhaps she would never know. But she knew that she would not forget to visit the church frequently to say prayers of thanksgiving for her deliverance, nor did she doubt that she would attend Confessional regularly, now that she knew who would be meting out her penance.

SADDLESORE

Jesse Morgan had a small spread outside of Nowhere, an aptly named town surrounded by vast acres of dry grass, thin cattle, and dour ranchers. The town itself wasn't much: one street, a saloon, a post office, and a dry goods store. I quickly left it behind, following the rumor that said the strange and enigmatic Jesse Morgan might be willing to hire a man for a few days. I intended to get enough money to get my ass out of Nowhere, then leave for anywhere, anywhere at all.

I was riding a bay horse with a limp, sitting in my well-worn brown saddle, equally worn leather chaps, blue jeans, a white shirt gone tan from the dust, and a ten-gallon hat to keep the sun out of my eyes. I felt as worn out as I looked, for I'd had no steady work for several months, and had been drifting, trying to find me a place to settle down. At least, as much as I ever settled down.

I spotted the house as I came over the rise, little dust clouds puffing up with each step my horse took. I reined in, and he stopped obediently. I watched the house for some time.

It was small and tan, made from adobe bricks made by the local Mexicans, with an orange tile roof. Practical for the region. The roof extended from the house, sheltering a deep porch that was home to a number of plants, which I supposed were medicinal in nature. I recognized the sword-like leaves of the aloe vera, but nothing else. I was never one for green stuff, unless it folded.

A single rider finally appeared, coming from the south, which was to my right. The horse was black with a white blaze on his face, and two white stockings. The rider sat tall and straight, with the easy erect carriage of one who is not merely a cowpoke, but a rider. Most waddies of my acquaintance stuck well enough to the saddle, but they rode with all the grace of a sack of potatoes.

The newcomer wore a flat-brimmed black hat like a rich Mexican, an embroidered black jacket, white shirt, with a flash of red at the neck. His pants were black, as was his saddle, though from the way it twinkled in places I knew it was inset with silver. A quirt was looped and fastened to his side. His hat brim lifted as he raised his eyes to me, but I sat still, neither waving nor shouting. I figured if he wanted to talk to me, he'd mosey on over. He didn't. He took the horse straight to water. Well, I had no complaints with that. A man depended upon his horse to make a living; and that was more important than some drifter.

He kicked his boots free from the long *tapaderos,* and slipped lightly to the ground. He was medium height, with a slim boyish build. He dropped the reins on the ground, and well-trained animal that it was, it didn't move. Those reins stayed put as if they had been nailed to the dry earth. He walked gracefully to the pump with only a slight rolling of the usual cowboy gait, and something nagged at me, something I ought to figure out, but couldn't quite.

He took a position at the pump where he could keep an eye on me, then started pumping the handle. Water splashed into the trough, and still the horse didn't move, though his ears pricked up and his muzzle flared. The young man came back, led the horse the last few steps to water, and let him drink. He stood watching me as I watched him.

I smiled to myself, for I liked this young man who looked to his horse and minded his own business, even when he had good cause to be inquiring as to the reason why a stranger had trespassed upon his land. I liked a thoughtful man, somebody who was slow to speak and who never had to take back words said in haste. You could depend on that sort of fellow. I dismounted and, conscious of my bow-legged gait, swaggered on down the hill, Ornery (that was my horse) ambling along with me.

"Howdy," I said, stopping about five yards short of the water trough. "Mind if I water my horse? It's mighty dry today."

He nodded, and I saw that he was not Mexican like his clothes, just tanned, with collar-length blond hair. He had no beard yet either, and I revised my estimate of his age downward.

"Help yourself," he said softly.

I walked past him, hands far away from the gun at my side. He wore no gun, but his black-gloved fingers caressed the braided-leather quirt, and I guessed he was probably pretty good with it. I'd tasted the whip on occasion myself, and had the highest respect for both a man who could use it and the damage it could cause.

Ornery was not so well mannered as the blaze-faced black. He pushed forward, shouldering past the slim youth, almost knocking him off his feet. In a surprise show of strength, he pushed back, forcing Ornery to sidestep—and landing on my foot. I swore, yanked my bruised toe out from under his hoof, and glared at the horse.

"You embarrass me, animal."

Ornery stuck his nose in the water with a fine disregard for my feelings. The black rolled his eyes and flicked his ears, but he kept drinking.

The young man kept a straight face, though his eyes twinkled. I was glad he spared my feelings by not laughing out loud.

"Yer pa around?" I asked casually, hoping the old man was as pleasant a person as his son.

He stiffened. "I'm Jesse Morgan. I own this spread." The voice was soft, but carried authority.

"You're Jesse Morgan?" I asked in surprise.

I looked him up and down real quick like. His nose had never been broken, and there were no scars on his face. His nose and jaw were prominent, and I thought to myself, "Breed." Not quite half-breed, because of the blond hair and light skin, but enough Indian to offend polite society.

"I thought you were older."

He smiled tightly, and there were some lines in his face. "I'm old enough."

"I reckon so." I'd accidentally insulted the man, so I decided I'd better move onto another subject. "I'm John Choice. I usedta be called Choysington, but most folks shorten it to Choice, and that's fine by me." I offered my hand.

He gave it a firm shake, and I noticed the signet ring he wore over his glove. "JM," it said. "Pleased to meet you, Mr. Choice."

"Ah, I ain't no mister. I work for a living. Which is why I came out. I heard you needed a hand for a couple of weeks."

He cocked his head sideways while he looked me over real good.

"I need to mend my fences. It's boring, it's dirty, and it's hard work. Are you willing to work?"

"I dunno. Are you willing to pay?"

He smiled slightly. "Ten dollars a week, and all the beans you can eat."

"Sounds fair to me."

"You're hired. Put your horse in the barn over there, then come up for supper."

He pulled up the black's head, and walked off to the barn with an easy stride that looked slow and comfy, but ate up the ground. Watching the way he glided along the ground gave me a nice tight feeling about six inches below my belt. He was younger than me by a few years, but he was no chicken. If I made a disrespectful move, he'd belt me for sure.

I grinned. Two weeks. Plenty of time.

■■■■

We rode the fence, finding the places where sand had just about buried the line, and planted new posts, braced by rocks. It was hard work, and hardly worth it.

"How many cattle you got on this spread?" I asked, holding the post straight while he piled rocks.

He sighed. "Too many and not enough."

I looked across the barren lands. "Yup. I can see that. So why here instead of some place more hospitable?"

"It's quiet. I inherited the land from my grandmother. She tried farming it and failed, and moved back to Texas. Well, I'm not too fond of Texas, so I came here."

He straightened and looked across the land. "And I do love it, even if it's not fit for man nor cattle. Just prairie dogs and birds. But folks mind their own business, and give a body peace."

I wondered what kind of trouble he had gotten into back in Texas. Wondered iffin maybe it was my kind of trouble. "Takes all kinds of folks to make a world. I figure what people do is their own damn business," I drawled.

He smiled appreciatively. "I'm glad to hear you say that."

My ears pricked up. I didn't want to tip him off if he didn't share my vices, but at the same time, I had to say something to find out if he did.

"I've been in a mite of trouble myself."

His blue eyes twinkled. "I'm not surprised."

My eyes met his, and there was a knowing look there that made my heart skip a beat. But just what did he think he knew about me? Then his mouth covered mine and I quit worrying, because he was a hell of a kisser.

The first touch of his mouth was soft, like sinking into a featherbed. Then it was wet, as he licked our lips and my mouth popped open without any thought of mine. His tongue gently explored my mouth, and fire burned through my body, my nipples standing up hard against the rough shirt, my breath coming in quick little pants. It had been an awfully long time since I had kissed anybody, and I was desperate to make the most of it, while at the same time scared I'd blow it if I moved. So I held still, and let him do what he wanted, willing to go along with whatever he had in mind.

He lifted his mouth, and smiled at me, crow's-feet appearing at the corners of his eyes. "Did you like that?"

"Yessir, I sure did."

"You wanna do it again?"

I didn't trust myself to speak, so I nodded.

His eyes twinkled and he straightened up. "Later."

He walked away, sinking to his ankles in the sand, leg muscles flexing as he slogged through the soft stuff. I caught my breath, and wished my pants were about two sizes bigger, because they had suddenly become awful tight.

"It's gettin' late," Jesse said. "We might as well camp here. No point in going back to the house when we'd just have to come back in the morning."

"You're the boss," I agreed.

He turned and looked at me with a funny kind of look. "You like being bossed around?"

My voice caught in my throat, and I nodded. I thought I should say something to take the strangeness away, but his eyes were glowing at me, and he nodded.

"Thought so," he said in a matter-of-fact voice. "Will you do what I tell you?"

"Yes, if it's fair," I answered reasonably enough.

"What if it's not fair?"

I felt my knees grow weak, and a strange yearning swept through me. "Yessir," I whispered in response. "That too."

And then I was scared witless, because I'd played some games like this before, but never with anybody as smart or as sharp as Jesse Morgan. His eyes dropped to my crotch, noting the bulge in my pants, and he smiled again.

"I like a willing worker."

I thought I'd die of embarrassment, but he said, "Get my saddle. Put it on that rock over there."

He waited impassively, waiting to see what I'd do. I wondered what I'd do too, then found myself walking over to the black. I spoke softly to the animal, tossed the stirrups over the seat, and uncinched the belly bands. It was a gorgeous saddle, black leather, tooled all over with roses, leaves, and thorns. Here and there silver was inlaid, and shone dully under the dust. The stirrups were hooded with long *tapaderos* in the Mexican tradition. I paused for a moment, then heaved it into my arms. It was heavier than my saddle, and after a day of mending fences, my arms were a mite tired. I lugged it over to the indicated rock, a rock that was about three feet by one foot across the top, and about three feet tall. I noted some chisel marks where its shape had been improved by human hands. When the saddle flopped down over the top, he said, "Fasten the belly bands around the rock."

It didn't exactly fit that way, but the bands were long enough to reach around the ends and up again, buckling on the last hole of the girths. I noticed a certain amount of wear on that hole, as if it got used from time to time, and I got the inkling that I wasn't the first man Jesse Morgan had brought out here. That made me feel a little better, because he knew what he was doing, and it also made me a little more scared, for the same reason.

Jesse's silver spurs jingled as he walked up behind me and draped his arm over my shoulder. He held the looped quirt in his hand, and the loops of leather brushed against the front of my shirt, sending a shock of pleasure in a straight line from my nipple to my groin. I let out a gasp.

He rubbed the leather against my chest then, and I gritted my teeth to keep back a moan of pleasure.

"You like leather kisses?" he asked softly.

"Yessir," I replied breathlessly, all my mind on the feel of the leather rubbing my nipple through my shirt. Then he pinched my nipple between two loops of the quirt and the pleasure was so intense I thought I was going to fall. He put his other hand on my arm to steady me.

"Take off your hat, cowboy." I tore off my hat and threw it in the dust, not caring where it landed or what happened to it, even if it was almost new.

"Bend over."

I bent over the beautiful black saddle, letting out a cry that was half pleasure and half fear. I grabbed the stirrup leather and braced my legs, but Jesse had more in mind. He buckled the quirt against the curve of his hip again, and shook his lariat loose from the saddle skirt where it was tied. My mouth went dry and a bolt of fear went through me, and I gave him a pleading look, but he smiled tightly, and kneeling before me, looped the rough rope around my wrists, tying each of them firmly. Then he took the loop around the base of the rock, and around my legs, tying my boots together. I let out a long moan, then went limp, powerless to stop what was coming, and knowing I'd voluntarily let this strange man put me in this position.

He stepped up behind me, and I felt the heat of his groin against my backside, but he didn't touch me. He slid his hands under my belly, and manipulated the buckle of my gunbelt. I had completely forgotten it, but Jesse hadn't. He took it away from me, and I felt even more vulnerable than before. He came back and slid his hands under my belly again, this time unbuckling my belt, and unbuttoning my jeans. He untied my drawers too, and pushed the whole mess down inside my chaps so that my bare ass was hanging out. I rubbed my cock against the warm hard rock and spread my knees, cooperating with him as much as I could.

"Ready?"

"Yessir," I managed to reply.

The quirt bit like a snake, a small red welt growing on my backside, smarting like a son of a bitch. I jumped in place and yelled, and then it bit me on the other side and I swore. Snap, snap, snap, three quick lashes made me dance violently and I shouted, "You bastard! You horny son of a bitch! You—"

The feel of his black-gloved hand on my ass shut me up. He rubbed it down the crack, finding the wrinkled knot of flesh between my cheeks, and asked, "What did you say?"

"Sir," I said. "It hurts like the devil when you use the quirt on me."

"You like this better?" And he pressed on my asshole.

Pleasure shot through me, making me sag against the saddle. "Yessir," I moaned in reply.

"To get this," he fondled my asshole some more, "You have to take this." He held the quirt before my eyes.

"I can't," I said.

"You will," he replied.

He backed away, and the quirt flew again, and I wailed like a baby, knowing there wasn't a damn thing I could do about it. Tears ran down my face as welt after welt was raised on my ass. I danced the hot foot, weeping and moaning, feeling awfully sorry for myself and cursing myself for a fool when suddenly I realized that as much as it hurt, I could take it. I quit jumping around like a pea in a frying pan, and stood stock-still like Jesse's horse.

"That's better," he said. And the quirt hit harder.

No one had ever used me as hard as Jesse Morgan, and I liked it. The pain took on a new flavor, a flavor of desire.

I began to groan as each stinging blow landed upon my ass, my nerves on fire with pain and pleasure, the two of them twisted so tightly together that I could not imagine one without the other. Lust surged through my body, and I cried, "Harder!"

Jesse adjusted his stance, and now the quirt cracked viciously across my ass, and I felt the internal throbbing that meant I was close to coming. I moaned and begged, "More!"

The quirt snapped across my battered butt, the pain pushing me into an intensity of need I'd never known before.

The quirt landed once more, and my body rocked with spasms and I cried out, "Fuck me now!"

The quirt fell into the dust at my feet, and Jesse's fingers pressed hard against my asshole, forcing me open while I groaned and grunted. Four fingers sank to the knuckles, my muscles quivering and twitching at the unaccustomed fullness. He held them there while I shook and moaned and came hard.

After a few minutes, I said, "Ouch." My vision refocused, and I remembered where I was, what I was doing, and who was doing it to me.

"What hurts?" Jesse asked.

I groaned. My ass hurt like hell, but the thing that was really bothering me was his hand in my ass. "I've never been fucked by anything that big before," I said.

He slowly withdrew his hand and I breathed a sigh of relief. He bent and dropped two gentle kisses on my abused flesh, then walked around in front of me.

"You've made me very horny," he said, stripping off the left glove, the one that had been in my ass. I looked expectantly at him. To my disappointment, he wasn't hard. After what he'd done to me, I'da thought he'da been hard as a rock.

"You haven't figured it out yet, have you?"

"Sir?" I asked.

He unbuckled his big silver belt, and I opened my mouth obediently. He slid the pants down his legs, revealing tan skin and a golden-haired pussy.

"Holy shit!"

I looked up at her. She smiled down at me. "Eat it," she commanded.

I never turn down pussy, even if I'm surprised by the offer, so I sucked her womanflesh into my mouth, tasting the musky flavor of her arousal, while her juices dripped down my chin. She groaned and arched her back, one gloved and one ungloved hand holding my head while she ground herself against my face. I sucked her little bump into my mouth and she thrust against my face, so I slacked off, then sucked hard again. She whooped like a bronco rider, and I sucked her harder. She smashed my face with her hairy mound, and I wasn't able to keep hold of her slippery bump, but I tried. Her fingers twisted into fists pulling my hair, and she pushed her wet sex against my face. She fucked my face hard, hips bucking like a man, my mouth the object she fucked, taking her pleasure from my bound body, while I tried to keep my tongue on her cunny bump. Fluids gushed from her hole, and she arched her back, suffocating me with her sex, and I grinned like an idiot, thinking to myself, "It doesn't get any better than this."

After a moment she said, "I think you like being used this way."

"Yes, ma'am, I sure do."

She slapped my face lightly. "That's 'sir' to you. Not a person within ten miles of Nowhere knows what you know."

"Yes, sir!" I replied.

She hitched up her pants, then walked around the rock and stroked my damaged hide. I twitched with pain, but felt my cock bob in anticipation of what else she might do to me.

She slapped my welted ass, and I flinched, a groan escaping my lips. "I think I'll keep you."

"Sir?"

"You have any place better to go?"

"No, sir."

She slapped my ass again, harder. This time I bit back a groan and trembled.

"Do you want me to own you?"

Why not? I'd drifted for years, had my fun in saloons and around campfires, scrounged for work, been perpetually broke, and never been welcome in one place for very long. Her spread was a harsh and bitter piece of land, but it was hers, and it was peaceful.

"Yessir. I do."

"Good," she said with satisfaction. "I'm going to brand you now."

"Sir?" I screeched.

"You belong to me; I put my mark on you." She spoke matter-of-factly, and there was no arguing with her.

"Yessir," I replied meekly.

She built a small fire on the sand, then removed the signet ring from her finger. It was large, about an inch long by five-eighths of an inch wide. The initials JM were large and clear. She used a stick to hang it in the fire, and when it was red-hot, she fished it out again.

She showed it to me, the fiery red metal hanging on the green stick. I was mighty relieved it was such a little thing, and not a real branding iron. With her gloved hand she plucked it off the stick, then walked around behind me. I shook miserably in the ropes, and she said, "Hold still, or you'll mess it up and I'll have to do it again."

I stood stock-still, my heart clamoring with fear, my bare ass waiting for her brand. She slammed her hip against me, knocking me against the saddle, my body hanging heavily over the leather. With her hip pinning my ass in place, she forced her knee between my thighs so that my right leg was immobilized by the rope around my ankle and the pressure she put upon it.

I shrieked as the fiery metal kissed my ass. I had a little hair on my rump and I smelled it burning. I thought then that I would puke, but after about ten seconds she lifted the ring. She blew softly across the wound, the coolness of her breath soothing it a bit. A warm shiver worked up my spine, and I took a sudden gasp of air. I was owned. Owned, roped, and branded, by this strange and compelling woman. No more wandering from place to place, no more chasing tail, no more freedom. And I was blissfully happy about it.

"Sir," I asked. "Would you fuck me some more please?"

"With pleasure," she replied.

CLEOPATRA'S DOGS

n preparation for the visit of Marcus Antonius, twenty slaves swept, scraped, and polished the Queen's marble receiving room. Cleopatra supervised the work herself, and was freer with the crop than usual.

The atrium and antechambers were scoured in similar fashion. Lithe, golden carp replaced the older fish that had become bloated and pudgy on table scraps. The satin curtains were cleaned and rehung.

Finally, the Queen ordered new silk wraps and cushions in green and gold for the wide receiving-couch on which she would lie.

A crew of thirty Greek gardeners sweated in the botanical gardens that led off from the receiving room, excising every weed and trace of blight. When a hapless youth damaged a hibiscus, Cleopatra herself dragged him aside, pulled off his tunic and administered the punishment with her crop. Red weals glowed on his buttocks before she was done.

Warm inside and out, she allowed her maidservant Tiri to lead her away to her bath.

■ ■ ■ ■

"She's going to seduce me," said Marcus Antonius. "I'll wager good odds that I've had her by dawn."

"You're here for Rome," said Quintus Cornelius, his aide-de-camp. "So if you've got any sense you'll keep your dick inside your toga and behave like the General you are, or Egypt'll be the death of you."

Marcus Antonius was not offended—he and Quintus had shared many flasks of wine on the long journey to Egypt— but the time they had already waited in the Alexandrian antechamber was beginning to tell on him. He strode across the atrium and back again, mindless of the array of golden fishes in the pool or the squadrons of fresh and exotic flowers mustered in his honor. "You haven't seen her. You don't understand."

"No, I don't. I've seen her statue in the temple of Venus Genetrix in Rome a few times, and that'll suffice. You'd really consort with an Egyptian?"

"Don't be foolish," said Marcus. "She's a Greek. She's a Ptolemy in direct line from Alexander the Great. There's no drop of African blood in her veins."

"She's the Queen of Egypt and that makes her a bloody Egyptian, by my accounting," said the older man. "And I don't trust foreigners who aren't part of the Empire."

"You're an ass," said Marcus companionably. "Look here. My dick is my business. Cleopatra is my business. Sweet-talking her advisors is yours. Just do your job and stop bothering me." And he perched by the poolside and wag-gled his fingers in the water to make the fish scatter.

Quintus sighed.

■ ■ ■ ■

Two more hours saw Cleopatra bathed and scraped dry, her

skin luxuriously oiled and her makeup applied. Her body was perfumed richly: her arms with kyphi and violet, her breasts with orange blossom and jasmine, her calves with almond oil and honey, her feet with aegyptium and henna.

At last, as the sun dipped towards the edge of the high wall that surrounded the garden, Cleopatra reclined on the broad couch in her receiving room in a cloud of exotic scents. She breathed deep, her lungs filling with sweetness. Garlands cascaded from the Corinthian columns that flanked the room. Golden sunglow kissed the carpet of pink petals. She made a signal, and her handmaiden went to bring the Roman.

■ ■ ■ ■

"I first saw her right here, you know, in this palace, fifteen years ago."

"I know," said Quintus. "You were a staff officer, and..."

"And she was just a kid, but even then ... Lovely cheekbones, beautiful eyes. No chest at all, yet, but already she held herself like a Goddess. We never spoke, of course." Marcus chuckled. "I was way beneath her station. Then I saw her a couple of times in Caesar's villa across the Tiber when the old goat had her shacked up in Rome. Marvelous woman. Old Julius never let her out of his sight, and with good reason. Don't judge her by the statue, Quintus; she looks better pink than gold."

"Be careful, Marcus. She has ambition."

"Well, so do I ... What *is* she doing, to keep us waiting all this time? ... She kept me waiting at Tarsus, you know, after Philippi, when I sent for her—"

Quintus closed his eyes. Marcus did not notice.

"She came to me up the Cydnus River in a barge covered with gold, clothed as Venus Herself, and surrounded by beautiful boys, while her maids hauled on the ropes and handled the rudder. The music of flutes and harps swirled around her. Even the bloody *sails* were perfumed. And purple." Marcus laughed. "We had great conferences—she couldn't ignore me now, mind—and she proved herself innocent of giving aid to Caesar's assassins, and we ate and we drank and the boys sang and the girls danced like Naiads till the sun rose, and I had a hard-on that put the mast to shame, but not once would she meet me alone."

"Smart woman. Gods' sakes, Marcus, she's a protected sovereign, a client-Queen of Rome, not some senator's country niece with stars in her eyes. What did you expect?"

"Client-Queen? Egypt doesn't see it that way. Her armies think she's the daughter of Amun. In fact you're probably the only person for ten days' march who doesn't think her divine. D'you know she's the first ruler here for three centuries who speaks Egyptian and takes part in their religious ceremonies?"

Quintus leaned forward. "I don't doubt her power, Marcus. That's exactly my point."

Marcus leaned too, so his face almost touched his aide's. "And this is mine. I'm not a lovestruck boy with his first erection. I know exactly what I'm doing. This country is rich, richer even than Rome. It could be a bottomless source of supplies and armies and funds for mercenaries, but first I need to master the Queen. I've got high hopes for Cleopatra, Quintus Cornelius, and that isn't just my dick talking—hello!" This last was to a servant who had appeared at his elbow.

"Cleopatra the Seventh, Thea Philopater, Queen of Egypt, waits on your attendance," said Tiri.

Always a man, Marcus did not fail to notice her shape beneath the simple tunic and skirt; she had a slender waist, generous hips, and large and splendid breasts which were hanging free, not supported from beneath as was the Roman custom. He exchanged a knowing male glance with Quintus, and willingly followed her to Cleopatra's receiving room, leaving his aide sitting moodily by the poolside.

As Marcus stepped across the threshold, his senses were assailed by such a riot of scents and colors that he blinked and his head spun. Fragrance surrounded him and settled on his skin.

"Greetings to Marcus Antonius and to my Roman cousins," said the Queen. "Please approach us."

Marcus struggled to find his bearings. He was in a fine, tall room cornered with pink marble pillars, its white ceiling lined with ruddy cross-rafters. To his right, a door led out into a formal garden, ranked with trees and shrubs. Preserving the symmetry of the room, this door was balanced by a niche to his left, crested similarly with a gold lintel and alternating panels of green and sapphire. A warm dusk light spread from high windows around the ceiling. The floor was strewn with the petals of a thousand rose bushes. Across this sea, on a couch in the exact center of the room, lay the Queen.

Her clothing was simple, a robe of fine white silk, but her jewelry proclaimed her royalty; a heavy bead collar with an elaborate hawk's-head clasp, and bead bracelets about her upper arms. Around her head was a circlet of gold, inlaid with turquoise and adorned with two feathers signifying her relationships with the falcon-God Horus and Maat, the Goddess of Truth. She held a fly whisk in her hand.

Cleopatra was, quite simply, divine in her beauty. Her legs were long and flawless, her feet almost sculpted in their delicacy. Her breasts were moderate in size but of a perfect roundness. The merest hint of her nipples showed behind the gauzy silk that covered them. And her face ... High cheekbones, white teeth, hair straight and black to her shoulders. Her eyebrows were neatly shaved and stenciled, her cheeks rouged, her eyelids painted a deep green. Where her skin was bare, it shimmered with perfume and sparkled with gold dust.

Marcus saw, then, that Quintus had been right: her blood might be Greek but her soul was truly rooted in the Egypt of the pyramids and pharaohs. The light from ancient kingdoms shone from her eyes. He had felt this antique power before, coming at him from the faces of Celtic chieftains in transalpine Gaul, but the clarity and beauty that burned in Cleopatra was stronger yet. Rome seemed a stripling youth in comparison. He found himself studying every inch of her, while fate swirled around them.

"Do you speak?" she said, and he heard the music of a thousand instruments.

He pulled himself together. Where were his wits? She was just a woman. "I apologize," he said. "Your beauty steals away my tongue, just as it did at Tarsus."

"You were bold enough in Tarsus," she replied. "Almost."

Rose petals whispered about Marcus's calves as he waded across the room.

Her lips parted. Marcus saw a row of perfect teeth and the pink tip of her tongue, and felt his body respond to hers. What he had taken for heavy rouge was, in reality, enhanced by a deep and healthy flush to her cheeks. Her almond eyes were wide, her breathing shallow.

Unbelievably, he saw that the Queen of Egypt was floating in a warm pond of longing for him. Already. And he hadn't even done anything yet.

Tiri withdrew, and the doors closed.

"Sit by me, Marcus Antonius."

Through his daze and the surging of the blood in his veins, a soldier's nub of caution prodded at Marcus. "How can this be?"

She smiled and he sat. "I prepared myself for you. I wished to be memorable."

Her bare arm brushed the back of his hand. His fears vanished. "I'm sure you will be."

Silk whispered as she raised her skirt. On another woman it would have seemed a coarse gesture. On Cleopatra it bound his breath in his throat. "We could blush and tease and be coy, like the common folk, if you would prefer," she said. "But that would waste time. People of our rank should be plain about taking what we need." The clasp that held his toga fell to the floor, and she drew back the layers of white cloth and slid his undergarments aside to gaze frankly at his nakedness.

He fumbled with her robe until she showed him the way. Her nipples were coated with gold. She raised her knees and he tugged till she rested on the edge of the couch, showing her neat, glistening pubic hair and the sweet roundness where her thighs and buttocks met. Words failed him again.

He entered her, and both cried out.

And then, Cleopatra pushed him away. "Onto the couch," she said. "I must lead, or you will be finished too speedily for me."

Marcus did not dispute it. He pushed himself up and lay down, the cushions cool beneath him. He stroked her creamy taut flesh as she knelt over him.

Her hotness engulfed him a second time. He thrust up against her weight, into her sweet core, as she straddled his hips. Cleopatra's backbone was straight and her balance superb as she stared down at him through slitted eyes and rode him like a fine horse. In the root and branch of him a slow pressure began to build.

The fly whisk was still in her hand. She flicked him with it then, a quick, stinging blow across his chest, and as his rhythm faltered he saw it was not a whisk at all. Set into the bone handle were nine thin leather thongs. It was a flail. A cat-o'-nine-tails.

The next blow was to his hips, nine tiny lines of pain. His cry was wordless and indignant.

"The Roman women do not teach you control," said Cleopatra, her words punctuated by her long thrusts. "I am disappointed in them." The flail scored his chest.

"Stop it!" He reached up to seize the weapon from her, but she leaned back and accurately whipped his forearm.

"Down," said the Queen. She had stopped moving against him, and her weight pinned him to the couch. "Obey me."

The solid authority in her voice took the breath from his throat. He said nothing as she took his right wrist and leaned over him to place it against the silken couch above his head. A round breast kissed his cheek.

She touched the wrist with the flail's bone handle. "This arm is now bound." With his left hand she did the same. "This arm, too. Move them and you will be punished."

The head of his cock twitched helplessly. The blow from the cat struck his shoulders. "That, too, is disobedience, Marcus Antonius."

Marcus could easily have overpowered her, had he willed it. What held him back was his burning need for release, his unwillingness to lose the sweetness of her around his cock, and the hope that perhaps later she would act the slave for him in return. He could think of many delicious indignities to lavish on that beautiful body. "Next time, I may be the ruler?" he said through clenched teeth.

She raised her hips and began the sweet thrusting, torture that was almost sharper than the whip. "Perhaps."

It went on. To Marcus, it seemed that she rode him for an age. Her breasts bobbed, her hair swung, and he became so transported by her beauty and the powerful ballooning of his sensations that he lifted his hands to caress her again.

Punishment was swift. Her flail worked on his torso while the flat of her other hand struck the side of his rump in stinging blows until the muscles in her arm stood out. She forced him down, beat him back onto the marble, and he felt the contractions as her orgasm swept over her, brought on by the obvious joy of her domination even as the pain made him grit his teeth and pushed away his own finishing.

The crescendo passed. Red weals shouted from his body, and still Marcus could not reach his release. He forced his arms up again and seized her hips. "Me!" he shouted. "Me now!"

Tiri was there. Her breasts came into view over him and his hands were held in an iron grip. Cleopatra moved against him, eyes closed, the sudden gentleness bringing tears of frustration to his eyes.

She reached forward. Her fingernails were painted the same deep green as her eyelids. Lust, joy, and cruelty blended on her face.

Her nails jabbed his skin by the collarbone. She slowly dragged them back across his chest, past his nipples, his ribs, all along his drum-taut stomach to his pubic hair. She raised herself a little and the nails scratched his tight scrotum.

Tiri's full weight was on his arms. He was trapped beneath the two women and could do nothing at all for himself.

Behind the burning of his pain and desperation, he felt the bloom of a perverse pleasure at his own helplessness.

Cleopatra bent and licked the sweat from his chest. Her teeth scraped his nipple.

"What am I thinking of?" she said. "You are my guest. Release his arms, Tiri, and assist me. As for you, Marcus ... *Nephthys.*"

He did not recognize the word, but her meaning was clear. Free at last, he drove himself up into her with all the force his suffering muscles would allow. He bucked on the couch, beyond thought, clasping Cleopatra's breasts in his hands, rolling the tight golden nipples in his fingers. Cleopatra's hands were on him too, and her hips pounded back at him with a force equal to his own. He could smell his own sweat, and roses, almonds, oranges. Gold dust fluttered from her body and he felt her contract and pulse and flood again, eyes and mouth wide, as the sharp knife of release scored him from the base of his shaft to the boiling giant tip of him and he exploded inside her in a huge, grunting cry.

Cleopatra tumbled onto the couch beside him. Marcus's heart thudded like the drum that set the time for the rowers of his Imperial ship. He swallowed air.

His penis was soft now. He touched it gently, teasing the last echoes of sensation from it. Spent for the moment, he knew it would not be enough.

Though his wounds smarted, Marcus was prepared to be magnanimous. "I see you were prepared for me. A sumptuous greeting."

"A fair beginning to our alliance, Marcus Antonius."

The soldier in him awoke. "Alliance?"

Her fingers tickled the hair on his arm. "You need what only Egypt can grant you. An army at your back. Strength to face Octavian and the others in Rome."

With the embers of passion still glowing, Marcus was not ready for this. He also realized that their recent coupling had left him in a position of some disadvantage, if negotiations were about to follow. Better to wait until he could take the upper hand. "Ah, politics. What nonsense it all is."

Cleopatra's beautiful eyes captured him and swallowed him up. "Not nonsense, Marcus. We must talk and plan. But not yet, I agree. We barely know each other, after all. Tiri, serve our guest."

Tiri reappeared by his side, bearing an urn and cups. They drank honeyed wine mixed with water, and their perspiration cooled their skin.

As the slave girl refilled his cup and turned to leave, Marcus's eyes were drawn again to the size and gentle movement of her breasts under the thin cloth.

Cleopatra laughed. "I thought as much. Men speak love poems to me, but their gaze is always on my handmaiden. You want her, don't you? Ah, men are faithless." She flicked him very lightly with the cat. "Tiri!"

The slave stopped at the door.

"Be naked for our guest," said Cleopatra.

Tiri reached to her navel and the skirt fell to the ground. Marcus's eyes followed the smooth curve of her rump as it met her thighs, and noted the plucked baby-smoothness of her mound. Then the fabric fell away from her breasts.

Her areolae were pink and as large as Marcus's palm.

"Knees," said Cleopatra in her voice of command. Tiri sank slowly into the mass of petals until they reached her thighs.

"Come to us."

Tiri crawled a path through the rose petals, breasts swaying, her shoulders back to support their weight. Slowly she moved, so slowly that Marcus's penis had time to tickle and swell into tumescence by the time she knelt before them, her face calm. Cleopatra's beauty excelled all others in Marcus's world; she was a fine goblet where her servant was only a sturdy vase, but Tiri had an earthy appeal that excited him. While Cleopatra's essence was masked beneath layers of unguents and aromatic oils, the musky female smell of Tiri floated freely in the air and teased his nostrils. Her head was level with his waist.

"Give tribute."

Tiri leaned forward to place the gentlest, most sensuous kiss on Cleopatra's labia. Marcus saw the hint of her tongue against the Queen's most sensitive spot, and Cleopatra's brief shudder of desire.

Then, Tiri turned to Marcus Antonius.

He was fully erect again, and the breath scraped in his throat. Tiri's hair was coiffured and bound up to form a layered pile atop her head, dusted with powder. The curve of her ears was delicious, the rouge of her lips a promise, the sweet calmness of her eyes a taunt, her huge breasts an altar.

Her deliberate slowness was agony to him. He could not wait to feel her obeisance. He rocked forward and his cock slapped against her cheekbone, missing the pouting lips, which kissed only air.

Cleopatra's flail caught him in the hip, and a backlash across his balls made him gasp. "Rome has no patience," she taunted. "The Greeks run marathons, the Egyptians last from the beginning of time, but Rome merely sprints."

It was too much to bear. He snatched the flail out of her hand and threw it aside. "Rome can endure!" he snapped. "I can last any course you set for me!"

One perfect stenciled eyebrow raised itself, but otherwise the Egyptian Queen was quite still. The Sphinx itself was not calmer. On the floor before them her naked maidservant waited, breasts moving as she breathed.

They regarded him coolly, and Marcus Antonius began to feel a little foolish for his outburst. Her tone had been light and not accusatory, and he had just been favored beyond his hopes by this remarkable, flawless woman. He was a child, and deserved to be treated so.

Marcus reached into the sea of petals at his feet and fumbled until he found the flail. His tight buttocks were next to the slave's lips. He held the cat out to Cleopatra.

"Thank you," she said. "But you must take it now. I have these." She reached beneath a cushion and brought out a flat wooden paddle and a long supple cane. "You wish to prove you can last the course?"

Maybe he should not have spoken in such haste. Too late, now. "Certainly."

Cleopatra stood behind her slave and gave her a stinging slap to the rump with the paddle. Tiri gasped, and the Queen said, "Our guest wishes to savor his pleasure. Take him where he wishes to go, but start slowly, as slowly as the Sun-god sets over the Nile."

The beautiful mouth approached him again. Marcus stood stock-still. He would not earn the Queen's rebuke a second time, not if it took until dawn to receive his pleasure.

And it might. Cleopatra swung the paddle again and the smack echoed off the marble walls to be swallowed up by the rose petals. "Too fast," she said.

Slowly, slowly, Tiri's face approached. Marcus's stiff cock strained as if trying to grow the extra inches to close the gap. That mouth, so wide and heavy-lipped, promised sweetness beyond all but Cleopatra's own.

Her lips grazed his tip, and parted. Wet and warm, her tongue touched him. He made the faintest of moans as she slid herself over him.

Another slap. "Too fast again, wicked girl!"

Marcus saw a pink bloom begin on Tiri's rump. Her breasts tickled his thighs, then pressed against them, her nipples crinkling. She moved almost imperceptibly, and it took an age for her lips to meet the ridge where his foreskin met his shaft. He imagined enduring this for an hour, his pulsing hardness teased by that warm and willing mouth, and prayed that Cleopatra's patience could not stretch so far.

He moaned again at the scent of her hair and skin. Perhaps Tiri knew his need, for he felt her tongue begin to flutter against the sensitive tip of his cock, her movement all but concealed by those smooth cheeks.

Cleopatra was not fooled by the subterfuge. "Cease that!" she shouted and, dropping to her knees, applied such a barrage of slaps to Tiri's buttocks with her bare hands that Tiri grunted and eased back on Marcus so she would not fall against him. Marcus took the opportunity to rest his hands on her shoulders, but the feel of her smooth skin heightened his desire beyond his ability to bear it and he lifted them away again.

"Whip her," said Cleopatra curtly. "She is bad and wicked, and must learn obedience," so Marcus, obedient in his turn, raised the flail and brought it down on her back. The shock of impact sent a tingle up and down his body, and helped him resist the torture of the slave's mouth on him. He hit her again.

Cleopatra's paddle had a long thin handle, leather-wrapped. She reversed the paddle now and jabbed the handle roughly into the girl's behind.

As the first three inches disappeared inside her anus, Tiri's eyes grew wide and Marcus felt the vibration of her groan skip up and down his cock. He shivered with pleasure and guilty desire as Cleopatra pushed still further. Tiri squirmed, and there was a brisk crack as the Queen gave her a sharp blow across her buttocks with the cane. "Be still!"

Excited by the helpless pain in Tiri's eyes, Marcus leaned forward almost against his will to apply the leather cords to her fine, smooth skin. His cock bumped the back of her throat. It was more than he could stand, and he pulled back his hips and drove himself even deeper into her, his thighs buried in the cushions of her breasts.

The paddle being planted as deep in her rear as it would fit, Cleopatra stood and encouraged her slave with harsh blows of the cane across her buttocks.

Urged on from the front and tormented from the rear, the slave girl was now rocking forward and back, plunging herself onto Marcus with long wet strokes. His balls swung against her chin and he watched and gasped as the full length of him disappeared beyond her face. It seemed to Marcus that as Tiri's mouth yearned for him, her buttocks yearned for the lash of the cane, for she raised herself to receive the punishment and her face became quieter and more absorbed.

He felt the first ripples of release. The breath thickened in his throat. Eyes dreamy, the handmaiden sucked and rocked and licked him.

Cleopatra threw the cane onto the couch and wrenched the paddle out of Tiri's anus, pulling her back. As her mouth slid off Marcus's cock she cried out in frustration and tumbled backwards into the rose petals.

Marcus Antonius threw himself onto her body, crushing the delicate petals between them. Tiri whimpered to feel the floor against her sore buttocks, but her knees and arms came up to greet him, her hand reaching for his cock to guide him. His tongue drove into her mouth and he tasted himself there. He slid into her easily, and her hips rose off the floor as she met his assault and returned it; the seething rush of pleasure took him and bent him and made him roar, and he spent himself utterly inside her body.

It was over, but he could not stop. His stiffness broke but his lust did not, and he strained against her, pushing at her hips, and when that did not satisfy him he knelt over her, pinching her nipples, and shaking her breasts like a pair of naughty puppies, and when that was not enough he slapped them and pushed them together and finally buried his face in their softness and let himself be rocked by her harsh, ragged breathing. We are both the Queen's slaves, he thought. She uses us as she wishes, and we comply. But, how sweet it is!

He heard Cleopatra say, "Very good, Marcus, very *sincere* and thrilling to watch, but I think you did not *completely* satisfy your new friend."

The Queen was standing with the cane in one hand and something small and white in the other. "Up, girl, and onto the bed," she said, and Tiri rushed to her knees, kissed her mistress's feet, and leaped up.

Cleopatra handed him a sculpture in porcelain, long and white, in the shape of an erect penis.

"The bars, Tiri."

The maidservant reached behind and beneath the couch, reappearing with two stout bars in her hands, equipped with leather shackles at each end.

"Marcus, if you would bind the victim?"

Tiri slipped her ankles through the leather cuffs, the bar holding her legs wide, and Marcus drew the cords tight and knotted them. Cleopatra restrained her arms with the second bar in similar fashion. Tiri lay spread-eagled and helpless on the couch, but Cleopatra pushed against the bar to force her legs even wider and expose the thick lips of her labia. "Open her," she commanded, and Marcus reached across to part those lips again. Her clitoris protruded from its hood, a glistening, reddened stub.

To his surprise, Cleopatra placed her face between her handmaiden's legs. Her tongue flicked out to tease the girl intimately. Tiri's hips strained.

Cleopatra slapped the side of her buttock. "Control, Tiri, who is mistress here?" and the hips relaxed.

Urged by his host, Marcus leaned in next to taste the girl. Her rich musk filled his nose and her warm dampness anointed his lips and chin. He heard a whimper and, from pity, scoured her with his tongue to repay her with pleasure for what she had already endured. A dribble of sweetness exuded from her lips to bless him for it.

The porcelain cock appeared by his face and slid up inside the girl. Cleopatra pushed him aside. "Watch, and you will know why I chose her."

"I think I know already," said Marcus.

The Queen said, "There is more."

The phallus quickened in her hand, and she applied fast, even strokes that made Tiri's breasts quiver. "Watch her. Look into her face."

Marcus knelt by the bed to see her better. Her cheeks were flushed scarlet and she breathed little gales through parted lips but still her eyes were calm, even though she suffered through a barrage of thrusts to her sexual center, quicker and harder than any athlete male could achieve.

"She wants you to hurt her again," said Cleopatra.

"What?"

"Hit her. Tiri, you may break silence to tell him."

The girl's nipples crinkled. "Slap me again. Like before."

Cleopatra switched hands effortlessly without breaking her violent rhythm into the girl's dampness. Marcus stood and filled his lungs with the honest stink of her. Brackish musk rose from beneath her arms, and a sweet cat's sharpness from her sex, but he also smelled spices and powder.

His hands played sweet torture on her breasts. When he pinched her he left red blotches on her flesh. His limp member hung against the huge mounds as they rolled and quivered under his slaps.

Tiri breathed deeply through her nose, lost in pain and pleasure and utter concentration.

"At your leisure, say the word of release. The one I spoke to you," said Cleopatra.

Marcus looked into Tiri's eyes and saw no abjection, no pleading. She looked straight into his soldier's soul. Her hands at the ends of the iron bar were quite relaxed. He knew that she could lie there forever resisting the pressure of her own ecstasy, and he did not need to see her prove it.

"Nephthys," he said.

Tiri sprang into feverish motion. Her lips spasmed, releasing a single sob. Knuckles white, she rocked against her bonds and the stiff leather burned ridges into her wrists.

Her breasts were a tidal wave beating against the shores of her chin. She was wracked, drawn, shipwrecked, and expired against the rocks. The muscles bulged on her shoulders and thighs. Marcus saw foam between her legs, salt on her forehead. Tears squeezed from her eyes.

And Cleopatra rocked against her, finishing her with gentle deep thrusts, and leaned forward to kiss her on the lips. "Dearest Tiri, you're so beautiful when you come. And now; remember yourself." Tiri's face became composed and subservient, her limbs relaxing into the couch.

Marcus was moved to kiss the girl on the cheek, tasting her tears. He had not kissed a slave from honest affection since he was eighteen years old. Cleopatra was ice and air, but the girl was earth and fire, and resonated with his soul.

Tiri ignored him, because she had not been told to do otherwise.

"A treasure," he said. "A lovely thing."

The Queen took the porcelain phallus and wiped it on the silk of the couch. "She has control."

"Yes."

"You could learn something of this control, Marcus. I could teach it to you. Tiri is exceptional, but woman or man, anything can be done with patience and discipline."

Cleopatra held the phallus to Tiri's mouth and watched her reach for it greedily. Marcus faltered when he saw it slide into her throat, but her face was joyful. Then Cleopatra tilted the urn into the broad end of the porcelain thing and wine streamed from its tip. Tiri's throat bobbed as she eased her thirst, and at her other end the wetness still trickled from her thighs and anointed her legs.

"I would like to have such patience," said Marcus, and wondered if he knew what he was saying. He was a leader of men, not a follower of women.

"It is not *you* who would need the patience," said Cleopatra. "It is your teacher who would require it." Her hand strayed between her own legs. The middle finger disappeared. "Well, we shall see. But for now, Marcus, as you're standing to attention so nicely, you have other business to attend to."

They coupled again, and this was the way of it: Cleopatra knelt on all fours over the supine body of her maidservant, knees spread to either side of the girl, their breasts pushed together, while Marcus knelt over them both and thrust into the Queen from the rear, steadying her with his hands, Tiri kissing her mistress's face and licking her ears and neck, her hands moving and teasing everywhere, the porcelain cock buried between the Queen's buttocks to the hilt and nudged deeper with every thrust Marcus made. Twice spent already, he endured through two of Cleopatra's shuddering climaxes until she laughed and pulled away, and turned to take his aching wet cock in both her hands and rub it sweetly, licking at his tight stomach muscles, until at last he achieved his pleasure and spurted his white seed in a trail across Tiri's golden breasts.

And even then Cleopatra would not let him rest, but scooped up his limp cock and scraped her nails across his scrotum, calling "Four! A fourth shot!"

But Marcus seized up a wine jug and bolted for the gardens and the cool evening air. "Enough! Or you will have to send my body back to Rome in a box!"

The Queen let him leave. "Not in a box, Tiri, I think," she said. "Perhaps at the head of an army of Egypt." She loosened the leather shackles, but the girl still lay there, as she had received no instruction. "Enough, be yourself."

Tiri giggled and wiped her breasts clean with a handful of petals. Gone was the attitude of obedience as she said, "No more mercy for our guest tonight. You make it too easy for him."

"So far, yes. He's a strong man, used to leading. Being led is new to him, and I must be subtle. But his training has begun. He's already a different man from the peacock who entered our chambers this afternoon."

They kissed deeply, then sat and drank wine in companionable nakedness.

"I think he likes us already, a little."

"And I think he has a fine cock, once the newness is beaten out of it," Tiri replied. "But you'll spoil him, I tell you."

"All right, I agree. No more indulgences for Rome."

"Rome, or Antonius?"

"Both," said Cleopatra. "Both."

"You think he will march on Rome, for your sake?"

The Queen smiled. "I'm sure his thoughts have already turned in that direction. Rome is destined to be governed by Emperors, not councils and Consuls and triumvirates. The peace between Octavian and Antonius has always been uneasy. One will kill the other, in time."

Tiri rubbed Cleopatra's shoulders and neck. "But once Marcus is your slave, will he still be fit to lead armies?"

"Of course. Being dominated will give him a keener sense of how to dominate in his turn."

Tiri looked doubtful.

The sound of barking dogs sailed in on the night breeze.

"The pack has found him," said Cleopatra. "We should go and rescue him, I suppose."

Tiri's hands closed over the Queen's breasts, and she gave a little shiver. "Well ... in a little while."

■■■■

From the pool at its center, the garden spread outward in waves of orchids and shrubs. The chirping of insects brought peace to Marcus Antonius as he wandered between the flowerbeds, naked and replete. The natural setting complemented his feeling of rebirth. Something new had taken place tonight, he realized; accustomed to being in total control of his sexual adventures, he had yielded up the initiative, and it had been good.

Far from being alarmed at what he had lost, he reveled in his gains. There was a certain freedom that came from giving the reins to another, and the pain he had suffered had led only to a more rich and satisfying pleasure. Maybe he would winter in Egypt, assessing its troops and building alliances in the East, and learning control from Cleopatra.

A dog barked.

Beyond the trees he found a clearing with low seats. Climbing vines sprawled across a high trellis over his head. He sat.

The still of the evening had given way to a dry flurry of almost inaudible activity. Shadows moved just beyond his sight. A snuffling sound issued from behind a hedge.

Dogs. Did attack dogs guard the arbor? Why had the Queen not warned him?

Wine jug held like a club, he stood up on the seat.

They boiled into the clearing, around the trellis walls, through the hedges, growling and panting. He looked down on a sea of backs; white, black, brown. Two snuffled at his feet from opposite sides of the seat. One, farther back, barked openly. Several more sat on their haunches and inspected him.

Not dogs. Marcus saw Thracians, Hebrews, Syrians. The two worrying his feet were Upper Egyptian and Nubian. A Roman sniffed the rump of a Celt.

A Jew cocked his leg on the trellis and let go a stream of hissing urine. A Greek sniffed with interest, head lolling.

Men, on all fours, each with a collar.

Marcus felt his gorge rise.

"Romans!" he cried. "Get to your feet! Where is your pride?"

The Egyptian bit his ankle and he tumbled onto the seat. The nearest dogs scattered at the commotion, but the Nubians and Thracians bared their teeth and crept forward.

Marcus said, "I'll break the skull of the first man who comes near, and the neck of the second."

He was encircled by twenty slavering human hounds.

"Cleopatra!"

"Marcus." She stepped into the clearing, clothed once more in her beads and headdress. In one hand she held the leather paddle, in the other, a much longer, meaner looking cane than he had yet seen. A broad leather belt around her waist carried a coiled whip. At her heels came Tiri on hands and knees, a collar around her neck and a collection of rings and chains held in her mouth.

Marcus Antonius was outraged. "What have you done to these men? How dare you subject Roman citizens to such treatment?"

"They are my pets, Marcus, and my trophies. I treat them well. If they're good dogs, that is."

Several dogs sniffed at Tiri. She growled and bit the nearest on the shoulder, sending him howling.

"Five nearest, attend to me," said Cleopatra, and immediately she was surrounded by man-dogs licking at her legs, her belly, her pubes, and buttocks. A flush crossed her face and she staggered. "Dogs are so loving and affectionate, Marcus. Maybe if *you're* a good dog we'll get you a pack of bitches just for yourself. Or just ... ooh ... make you run around with your friends, here. Ah, enough, darlings, I can barely stand as it is." She smacked the cane against the flat of the paddle and the dogs relented.

"I will *never* be like *that,*" said Marcus in horror.

"I was joking, Marcus, really—I would never put you with the pack. You're of my class, and we will be companions, my word on it. But I'm afraid you *will* have to learn obedience. I won't be argued with in this way. Tiri, be a woman again and apply the cuffs."

Tiri stood on her hind legs and held a leather band and chain towards his wrist.

He thought about it.

She wanted his pain and his obedience, and when she felt he had earned it she would give him pleasure. It was slavery of a sort, and he rebelled against that idea, but to be made Cleopatra's plaything, submit to her will ... it was also a freedom beyond anything he had known. And after the initiation was over, he would be her companion, and her ally.

He slid his hand into the cuff.

A Parthian licked Cleopatra's foot unbidden, and she snapped the crop across his behind, making him whimper and scurry for the safety of the pack. Marcus wondered what that cane would feel like against his own skin and a warm thrill sent goosebumps down his legs.

Tiri finished the job of securing his wrists and neck. The chains led to ringlets, and as the pack watched, the maidservant fastened the wrist cuffs together to a rope that she looped over the trellis and made fast to a ring set into the ground. He was almost suspended, hanging before them.

"You did ask to learn, remember," said the Queen, walking around him, touching him with the cane, lifting his cock and balls with the flat of the paddle. "Tiri, bounce this a little."

Marcus Antonius looked within himself and found that, yes, he was ready for this, as Tiri knelt in front of him and subjected his cock to stinging blows, left and right between her palms.

Then the long cane whipped against his exposed buttocks. Red pain lanced though his spine. He screamed aloud.

"Come, that was gentle. I hardly raised a mark. You must take your punishment in silence."

"Gentle?" said Marcus.

The cane's tip found his tender anus and scraped inside, sending flame into his bowel. "'Silence,' I said, Marcus. Do you understand the word?"

Marcus, about to answer, caught himself and nodded instead.

"Very good," said Cleopatra. "But you had to think. Tiri, take the paddle." The cane landed again and again, and Marcus's feet lifted off the floor as he tried to escape the agonizing blows. Tiri spanked him next with the paddle, right over the sore stripes left by the cane, and his buttocks glowed. Like a pendulum he swung back to Cleopatra, who gave him three swift lashes with the cane, all exactly aligned on his thighs. She used such force that her arm muscles bulged.

"He does us homage," said Cleopatra. The Roman's cock was stiff and rigid, despite his wet cheeks and face white with pain. The Queen knelt and kissed him, and pulled his foreskin back. Even that touch made him sob. The glans beneath was slick with his fluids. Cleopatra's tongue flicked out, just once, to curl around the naked head of his cock, then she reached around his body to sink her nails into his flayed buttocks while his broken wail of anguish danced in the air above her.

Even in the hideous pain there was something he needed, something he drank up. He would show her his courage and make her proud. He would earn her devotion, even as he gave her his own.

Then the cane scored his tender buttocks again, and his resolve splintered. He sucked in his lips to avoid sobbing.

Cleopatra was in front of him again, her face just below his. Her beauty was like a balm on his wounds. She said, "It will be a long night, Marcus Antonius. Your aide has gone back to your ship. It will be just us, until dawn. Until you are tamed and kneel before me and beg to be allowed to kiss my feet."

He knew it was true.

Marcus took up his pride and his dignity and let them both go. The relief was almost exhilarating. He was an empty vessel for her to fill. The dogs were her evidence, witnesses to her strength and power, and Marcus felt himself giving way to her, wanting her, but wanting most of all to please her.

To hear himself say the words, regardless of any punishment he might earn, he said, "You are my mistress. All I want is to please you."

"You do not mean it yet," replied Cleopatra, "and it is wicked to say things you do not mean. Tiri, you may speak to explain it."

"Pain will always be pain, and you will never become accustomed to it," said Tiri. "But always there will be pleasure with it, and soon the pain and the pleasure will be the same, and you will learn that each is sister to the other, and yield yourself up without resistance. And that is the sweet moment, and after it everything is changed. And *then* you will gladly kneel, and mean it."

The dogs paced around the Roman's body. Marcus tested his bonds, but he was firmly held.

"Without the pain, he cannot understand." Tiri went to her knees and, a dog again, snuffled at the trickle of blood upon his thigh.

Cleopatra uncurled the whip from her belt. "Then, we will *make* him understand."

Erik Buck

NOBLESSE OBLIGE

Old Shedeur, my father's trusted advisor, reminded me: "My Lord Harald, tonight you must exercise your *droit de seigneur;* you must deflower a bride."

I was aware that lords do that, but I had been serving my uncle, Sir Einar, as squire, so I had never seen it done. When we learned of my father's untimely death, it was necessary that I cut short my training in courtly ways and return home, to take my father's place as lord. It was all rather overwhelming, being responsible for the castle, and the villages and estates, which are worked by hundreds of villeins, bordars, cottars, burs, and serfs. I replied to Shedeur: "I'm bone weary. I've been in the saddle most the day, and I am ready for rest. I suppose she must be sent to my bed chamber. Make it soon. I need a good night's sleep."

"My Lord Harald," Shedeur said, "it is not quite that simple. To do it correctly, it will take you most of the night. It will take some effort. You will work up a sweat, if you do your duty well."

"It's that involved? My father, may he rest in peace, used to take care of deflowering brides. Is there something I don't know? Can't I just stick it in her, break her maidenhead, and be done with it?" I would not, of course, admit that I had never stuck it in any woman, virgin or not. My experience was limited to younger boys, whom I could bully.

"By tradition, my lord," explained my mentor, "it's rather more involved than that. The custom of the lord deflowering the bride is ancient, and it serves several functions, to maintain the fabric of our society. As with any formal social ritual, it behooves the enlightened ruler to perform it solemnly and well." Of course, I was anxious to be an enlightened ruler.

"Well, Shedeur," I replied, "we'd better get on with it. You can talk me through it, can't you? I must admit, I have never deflowered a woman before." Truth be known, under Sir Einar's tutelage, I had never even lain with a woman. I was entirely ignorant of the pleasures to be found in them.

Shedeur led me to a tower, beside the main gate, and to the flat roof, from which, in war, archers could shower arrows down upon approaches to the gate. Standing at a crenel, I watched as the town's people escorted the newly wedded couple from the steps of the church, across the square, to the main gate of the castle. They saw my face at the battlements and assembled in a half circle around the base of the tower. The groom, a strapping lad, bigger than I, stepped forward, knelt, and then rose to speak: "My lord, I, Dragor, your loyal subject, request permission to ask a favor."

"Speak, Dragor."

"My lord, if it pleases you, I would send my bride, Else, to receive your favor. This I request, in accord with the ancient tradition."

"Your request is granted, loyal Dragor," I called down.

"Very good, my lord," said Shedeur. The crowd cheered.

Soon, my chamberlain brought the bride to me, her long hair tied with colored yarn and adorned with flowers, her coarse dress newly washed. Even her bare feet were clean. She was a comely lass, slim, yet well muscled. I rather suspect her father had used her to pull his plow. She stood, with downcast eyes.

"You are Else?" I said, not quite sure what I should say.

"Yes, my lord."

"And you wish me to ... prepare you for your husband, Dragor?"

"Yes, please, my lord."

"Look at me, Else."

She raised her eyes and stared at me with what might have been devotion, or awe. Her features were not as fine as those of some of the ladies I had seen at court, but she was attractive to me. My member stirred under my tunic. I took her by the hand, and showed her to the crowd, below. There were more cheers. Then we retreated to the center of the space, where none could see us but my chamberlain and Old Shedeur.

The sun was low, and it glinted off her hair, gave a rosy glow to her face. She smiled at me. My chamberlain said, "Else, take off your clothes." Else unlaced the bodice of her woolen dress and began to pull the dress off, over her shoulders. Though her face and arms were tanned by work in the fields, her breast was pale. She stepped out of her dress and stood before me, naked, her hands at her sides. There was none of that covering up, trying to hide her breasts and crotch, that I might have expected. The low sun accentuated her curves, and the shadows emphasized how her young breasts jutted forth, how round was her belly, how full her thighs.

As a squire, I had not been permitted the company of women. My eyes roamed over her ripe body, drinking it in. My member stirred under my tunic.

"Where will I bed her?" I whispered to Shedeur, "I don't see a bed." The chamberlain went below, to fetch the bed, I assumed. "Must I do it here? In the open?"

"Yes, my lord, so that the people may hear the confirmation of the deed."

I could not keep my eyes off her, nor my hands, either. I stroked her breasts with my fingertips, squeezed them gently, as if they were ripe fruit. Her nipples, I noted, swelled and stood forth. I know now that it might have been the cool air which erected them so, but at the time it seemed a minor miracle. My hands ran down over her ribs, her hips. Very gently, I touched and examined her womanly cleft, between her legs, noting the curly hairs, which gleamed as if bedewed, for I had turned her to the sun, the better to see. "She is a fine wench," I said. "Where is that bed?" Else smiled at me.

"My lord," replied Shedeur, "there are some preliminary tasks to perform, first, for the benefit of her husband and her relatives." It was hard for me to pay attention, as I was fondling her girlish breasts and running my fingers through the intriguing mass of hair where her thighs joined her body.

The chamberlain came back, not with a bed but with a wooden post, to which was attached a crossbar, across the top, like the letter T. He returned again with bags of paraphernalia. From one bag, he took a rope.

To my surprise, Else thrust her arms forward, wrists crossed. She knew better than I what was to happen. The chamberlain bound her wrists together, leaving a long tail of rope. "I don't understand," I said to Shedeur.

"First, my lord," Shedeur went on, "you cause her great pain, so that she screams, for all to hear."

"Why, Shedeur, should I wish to cause her pain?"

"My lord, let me try again to make you understand," he replied. "Custom requires that you make it a unique, exquisite experience, one of absolute domination of the woman."

"Well, then, afterward you can give her a potion of forgetfulness, right? I can't go around inflicting lasting pain on perfectly innocent subjects. Were she a criminal..."

"No, NO. She must remember every detail. She must cringe in terror at the very thought of what you did to her, wake screaming in the night, when she dreams of it."

"Why, Shedeur? Why should I ruin this poor wench?"

"Let me explain, my lord," he said patiently. I could remember him lecturing me when I was a boy. I recognized the tone of voice. "First, of course, you do this thing to prove to the community that you can. It is your right, as lord, to have the first fruits, and you must exercise your right to retain it, to be seen to be acting as lord. Should you return her to her husband with no outward signs of your dominion over her, no wounds, no bruises, there would be no evidence that you even cared to exercise your right."

"Well, surely, Shedeur, a torn maidenhead is evidence enough."

"My lord, she can hardly display that to her friends and family!"

"Ah, I see your point, but need it be painful? Could you not give her one of your wonderful potions, that she should not feel the pain? Or make her forget?"

"Forget? My lord, this will be the most memorable night of her life, to spend the night as the object of her lord's attention. Why should she want to forget?"

"But, then, I should be gentle and kind, so she will remember me as a benevolent ruler," I argued.

"My lord, peasants are like animals," he explained. "You have seen how, among the animals, the males fight, and the winner, the most powerful male, gets the females? The victorious ram gets all the ewes. It is the way of Our Divine Creator to assure the betterment of the breed. The ewes want to be serviced by the strongest ram.

"It is the same with women. They have an instinct to be the sexual object of the strongest male. As lord, you are, by consensus, the most powerful male in the region—socially powerful. Any wench in your domain will willingly warm your bed, for you are the dominant male, with the power of life and death over them. Is that not so?"

"Yes," I admitted. "often, women of low station have approached me, unbidden." Of course, Sir Einar would never let me touch them. "Yet, I suppose, if I were a goatherd and not a lord, women would not be attracted to me."

"Exactly so, my lord," said old Shedeur, rubbing his hands and obviously pleased that I understood. "This peasant girl, Else, will want to remember that she was deflowered by a strong, powerful man, one so powerful that he could inflict any punishment, any degradation, at his whim. You must show her you are physically powerful, strong, dominant, heartless. You must show her that you care enough, care even about the humblest of your subjects, that you will exert yourself, all night, if necessary, to make her wedding night memorable, and leave scars to remind her. She may never lay eyes upon you again, but she will remember her one night with her lord. Secretly, she hopes you will impregnate her, so she may bear the strong son of a powerful lord, even though she is of the most humble station."

"But Shedeur," I said, "this husband of hers, Dragor, will he not resent being delivered his bride in damaged condition?"

"No, my lord. He will expect it. These peasant girls, even as the ladies of the King's court, have been raised to think of their virginity as their most treasured possession. There is always some resentment toward the man who takes it. There is always some feeling, deep inside them, when they couple with their husbands, that they are being used, abused, raped, if you like. You must use and abuse Else in so horrific a manner that anything Dragor may do with her in the future will seem gentle and kind in comparison. He will thank you for that."

Shedeur continued: "When Else suffers the pains of childbirth, will Dragor want her cursing him for inflicting that pain upon her? No, he will want to be assured that she will think back to this night and realize that the pains of childbirth are as nothing, compared to the pain you inflicted upon her. She will remember how her husband was kind to her, how he helped to heal her after her ordeal in the castle, and she will love him the more. You owe it to Dragor to be thorough, tonight."

"*Noblesse oblige*, I suppose."

"Yes, my lord, you must be seen to do your duty."

While all this was being explained to me, the sun was setting, so that now Else stood, patiently, bathed in the red glow of the sunset. Torches were brought to brighten the scene, and a brazier of glowing coals. The chamberlain fitted the wooden post into a socket in the floor and led the girl, Else, to it. He bound her ankles to the rings in the floor, so that her legs were spread wide. Then he drew on the rope which bound her hands, so that she was pulled over, against the crossbar, which bore against her upper thighs. She bent at the hips, and her arms were pulled taut before her, as the rope was fastened to a cleat on the wall. With all of this, she cooperated, making no protest, struggling not at all, though it must have been uncomfortable, with her legs spread so wide, and her body horizontal. Her hair hung down between her outstretched arms, and her breasts hung free, like ripe fruit. I went to her and held her breasts cupped in my hands. She turned her head and smiled at me. I stepped behind her and squatted, so the globes of her buttocks, stretched taut by her strained posture, were right before my face. So spread was she that I could easily see her little puckered shit-hole and below that the vertical groove of her maidenly cleft, the haired lips swelling, utterly exposed.

With my fingers, I parted her flesh, revealing her inner lips and pinkness. Gently, for I had never touched a woman thus, I moved my fingertip across her pinkness, exploring what I found. Farthest forward, I found a little lump of soft flesh, and when I pressed upon it, Else gave out a mewling sound, like a hungry kitten. It seemed, as if before my eyes, her cleft grew damp, even wet. I spread the inner lips and peered within, as the chamberlain held a torch near. "Tell her husband, Dragor, that his bride was truly a virgin." Not that I would have known the difference. I pushed my finger against her elastic membranes, marveling at the wetness, and marveling that I was touching Else's most private place. I was, no doubt, the first man to do so. I could smell her womanliness. Looking between her spread thighs, between her hanging breasts, I saw her upside-down face smile at me.

"My lord," said Shedeur, handing me a whip, "unless you would prefer the branding irons."

My heart raced, and I stepped to a wall, to clear my head, to take a deep breath of the evening air. I saw half the village, it seemed, standing, waiting beneath the tower, casting long grotesque shadows as the sun set. A murmur arose when they saw me standing in the aperture.

Almost automatically, I waved to them and turned away. Clearly, my subjects expected me to perform. I resolved to do my duty, to apply myself to the job at hand.

The chamberlain spoke, loudly and formally: "My lord, your serf, Dragor, presents his bride, Else, and prays you will exercise your *droit de seigneur.*"

The whip was in my hand, like a sword. It extended from me, the length of my forearm, stiff braided leather. Then it divided into long leather thongs, with knots. As I pulled the lashes across my palm, I could feel that each knot embraced a metal weight. It was a whip to wring a confession from the most courageous man. What would it do to a mere girl?

I could hear the crowd, below, beginning to get restless. Someone shouted, "I knew it. The slut likes it. Not peep of complaint." Else heard it, too, and the expression on her face changed to one of great pain and anger. That made me angry. I swung the whip.

The next instant is burned into my memory, the sickening slap as the knotted lashes fell upon her clear, pale skin, the ends wrapping around her body to snap against her tender breast, the screech, the howl, of anguish, which emerged from Else and reverberated between the castle walls, the sigh, the murmur, which arose from the crowd below. Else's taut body undulated with her agony, as her breath rasped in her throat. I could see, across her back, the livid stripes where the lashes had abused her pale skin. There was a spot of blood, where one of the knots had whipped around her ribs and pierced the skin of her tender right breast.

Scarce had she drawn fresh breath than I swung backhanded, and again the instrument of torture slashed her girlish body, eliciting yet another cry of agony, leaving a network of stripes, setting her left breast to quivering. The effort of beating her seemed to me natural, like the countless hours of sword practice I had endured as a squire, hacking forehand, backhand, at a post.

I realized, then, that in my limited experience, for a squire is supposed to remain chaste, I had never had the opportunity, never had leisure, to do anything I might want to do with a woman, to have her body entirely at my disposal. I felt a sense of power, a sense of—maturity—that I had not realized as merely the son of a lord, or squire to a knight. I realized, that night, there on the tower, that just as Else was embarking on a new life, with a new status, wife, just so this ceremony would launch me on a new life. For the first time, I knew real power over another. I *felt* like a lord! I knew, with each swing of the lash, that I was the LORD, with the power of life and death! This woman was mine!

Shedeur stayed my hand. I shook to clear my head, when I saw what I had done. Else hung, limp, from her hips and hands. Her back, her ribs, her breasts, her buttocks, her thighs, all the pale parts from her knees to her shoulders, were shades of pink or red, and in places, blood oozed, where the knots had gouged her flesh. Her head hung. "I have not killed her, have I?" I said, not believing what I had done.

"She will recover her senses, my lord," said Shedeur, who must have seen a hundred of these ceremonies. "You have done well. The rabble are pleased."

I walked to the wall and looked down. The shadowy figures below, some carrying torches, moved excitedly, talking among themselves, almost in a festive mood. They seemed to be waiting, expecting more.

I returned to Else, lifted her head by her hair, and gazed, by torchlight, upon her tear-stained, weary face. Her eyes were closed; she was not aware of me.

My chamberlain handed me a flagon of wine, from which I drank, as the three of us stood watching Else slowly recover. At last, her body undulated, and she raised her head, gasping. Her beaten breasts swayed, as her bruised ribs expanded. I pulled her hair, lifting her face, and put my wine flagon to her lips.

She drank, and writhed her bruised body, her hips fixed by the wooden crossbar, her arms kept taut by the rope to the wall. I walked to her other end, where her bottom, raised high, and her widespread limbs bore the overlapping welts from my exercise with the whip. Her cleft gaped, gleaming in the torchlight. No longer a shy, innocent squire, I thrust my fingers against her, squeezing her tender lips, pressing that little nubbin between them. I showed no hesitation; it was my right, as lord.

"Now?" I said to Shadeur.

"As you wish, my lord."

I tore at my tunic, and my chamberlain helped me undress. Soon, I was as naked as Else, and my manhood stood tall. Her sheath was fully exposed, ready for my sword, and I quickly found the point to apply pressure. With a heave of my hips, I rammed my meat home. "AAAHH!" she screamed. I pulled back, then pushed hard again, mashing her bruised buttocks as I drove as deeply as I could. "OH! AH! UHNGH!" she cried, exclaiming with each thrust. The crowd, below, heard and murmured acclamation.

In those days, I was young and inexperienced. With a euphoric thrill, I shot my seed into her belly and withdrew from her hot wetness. She sighed and mewled, as if deprived. Instinctively, I thrust my fingers into her bloody hole and fucked her vigorously, until she heaved her hips and cried out piteously, "Ah, oh, AHHH, OHHH!" I could feel her sheath gripping my hand, and then she sagged once more, spent.

"Well done, my lord, well done," said Shedeur. "She'll not soon forget this night."

Despite the cool of the night, sweat gleamed on Else's breasts, and her nipples jutted out. She breathed heavily, as if I had beaten her again, with the whip. But she lifted her head and smiled at me.

Shedeur led me to her, until I stood with my limp, wet manhood practically touching her cheek. "Else," he said, "you must take it in your mouth."

Else did not protest, but did as he said, licking, kissing, sucking on my member until, to my surprise, it again stood tall. "My lord," Shedeur said, softly, "there remains one virginal place. You must use her as you would a page."

I was never one to shirk my duty. I again took my place behind her, but I aimed my thrust a little higher, pressing against her puckered rosebud until, suddenly, I sank into her body. My belly mashed her beaten buttocks, and she gave one, loud, cry of pain and anguish. Then she was quiet, except for excited gasps, as I fucked her forbidden hole. She was tight, and the friction was delicious, but I had to pound her tortured buttocks with countless thrusts until, at last, I spent my semen in her bowels. She did not show the signs of ecstasy that she had when I fucked her cleft with my hand, but she sagged, exhausted, hanging from her bound wrists.

"Is more required of me?"

"No, my lord," said Shadeur.

"You did very well, my lord," said my chamberlain. It occurred to me that, by morning, the whole castle might know how I had performed.

I looked down at Else, and I think, that moment, I loved her. I knelt and untied her ankles. I went to the wall and untied the rope which held her hands. Released, she folded downward, her hair falling to the floor, her scarred back bent, her head between her knees. I lifted her off the supporting crossbar and cradled her in my arms. Then I carried her to my room, walking naked through passages of the castle, my chamberlain behind me, carrying the clothes, Shedeur before me, holding the doors open.

"Leave me," I said, as I laid her on my bed, her blood spotting the sheets. Alone together, I kissed each bloody wound. Else, dreamy in her exhaustion, mewled and wriggled, and then she slept in my arms. At the dawn, I awoke with Else's warm little body against mine, her arms embracing me.

■ ■ ■ ■

I often think of Else, for she was my first. Since then, I have deflowered a hundred brides, and countless maids who have come to serve in the castle, and 'most every lone farm girl I might come across in my travels. Nothing quite excites the passions like a good whipping, and never has one been less than grateful.

Raven Kaldera

GALLAE

Jadviga was busy heaving rocks when the gods granted his request. Baurux's gang had traveled here from Salona, up the coast and overland to Delmatia, and he had gone with them. Although it was not quite the direction he had wanted to travel in, it was better than taking the Roman roads alone and unaccompanied, and Jadviga not a citizen. That had gotten him enslaved once, and shipped off to the Great City as a slave gladiator.

"Put thirty-one through thirty-eight over there, under the tree," Zagid, the fat owner of this house-turned-rock-pile wheezed. Jadviga sighed and hauled the stones the extra twenty cubits. It was the custom in Delmatia to number every stone in one's house so that when the tax collectors came from Rome, one could take the whole structure apart and then moan forlornly to the tax collectors about how terrible it was here, how everyone lived in grass hovels (hastily erected for the occasion) and how there was no wealth in

Delmatia at all. Then, after they were safely down the road, having extracted only a few coppers, one could reassemble one's house as if it was a child's toy, dig up the buried root cellar where all the finery was hidden, and go on with life. Of course, there was a great market for travelers with strong backs to do the actual stone-hauling. Baurux's entire gang had signed up, although Jadviga suspected that it was only a ruse for Baurux's real ambition, which was probably to rob the tax collectors.

He was just taking a break to get a dipperful of water and consider, yet again, if he wanted to have anything to do with attacking a tax man well guarded by a Roman centurion when the gods dropped a handful of Fate in his lap. Beyond the crest of the hill a sound began to make itself known: a sound of cymbals and drums and chanting. Zagid perked up noticeably. "They are early this year!" he exclaimed in his gutteral Illyrian accent. "Usually they don't show until after the tax collectors come through and we have rebuilt everything!"

Jadviga had ducked quickly behind a pile of stones. He had learned to do that rather frequently over the past year since his escape. Everywhere he went, he stuck out like a sore thumb—over six feet tall with blond hair and beard, obviously a Teuton barbarian. "Is it the Roman troops again?" he asked from where he crouched.

"Nay, nay, Jadvigus, it is only the procession from Cybele's temple at Mount Ida. You need not hide." The fat man chuckled; he had guessed Jadviga's uncertain status when he had hired him. "They only come to wait for the rebuilding, so that they may bless our new homes and start the sacred hearthfires." He winked at the tall Teuton. "They come every year with their procession, and they never tell the Romans, either."

Something chimed like a bell in the back of Jadviga's mind. "The temple of ... Cybele?" he whispered, standing. "The—the gallae?"

"Aye, then you've seen them before? Ah, yes, I forget, you've been to Rome."

Been to Rome indeed, he snarled inwardly. Dragged there in chains and left under a bale of hay in a much-bribed merchant's cart. Rome can be damned as far as I'm concerned. "No," he said slowly, in a accent just as thick in its own way as the Illyrian's, "it was before Rome that I saw the gallae. In Cyrene." And I kept the gift I got there ever since, all through the humiliation of my captivity. It kept me from madness. Jadviga's hand went to the small battered leather pouch about his neck on a thong, and remained there as the Cybellines crested the hill.

There were ten of them, ten and a donkey carrying a small golden statue of a goddess in a miniature temple pavilion. Their garments fluttered in the wind: women's chitons and pallae in fine saffron-dyed linen, embroidered flammaem over long, elaborately curled hair dyed with henna or bleached with mares' urine. Jeweled pectoral plates gleamed on their breasts, inlaid with religious scenes and symbols. Their faces were painted with cosmetics; kohl rimmed their eyes and emphasized lashes, and red paint rouged their lips. All ten danced about wildly, flinging their long hair about and chanting in high falsettos at the top of their lungs. A few were pretty enough to be taken for maidens without a second glance; the rest ranged from homely to one in particular who reminded Jadviga of the story of when Thor dressed as a bride in order to infiltrate a giant's stronghold.

Then he saw her, towards the end of the procession. She was trying to dance and shake a sistrum and keep the temple from falling off the donkey with one hand. Something that felt like a great convulsive fist reached up from his belly and grabbed him by the throat. He remembered her from Cyrene. There was no way he could ever forget her.

Her hair had been darker then, not reddened with henna as it was now, and she had been almost painfully thin, without the soft curves that showed under the saffron robes. He had walked into the middle of some celebration that he did not understand, and had been given a quick explanation by a cheering bystander. The gallae had come pouring down through the streets in a frenzy, lashing themselves and each other with braided whips until their blood dripped onto the ground. Townsfolk had knelt in the streets to touch it. Jadviga had stared, open-mouthed. "They are seidhr-kraefter!" he had cried out to his native informer, who was busy looking over the shoulders of other bystanders and at any rate would not have understood the barbarian reference. Jadviga knew the godhi seidhr-kraefters, the men who incarnated the corn god and then sacrificed their manhood; if they lived, they were allowed to wear women's clothes and rejoin the tribe as women. But he had had no idea that there was such a custom anywhere else.

The thin boy on the steps of the temple had stood, swaying, hands crossed over his chest. His hair was as long as a girl's, hanging over the shoulders as he was flogged over and over by two older gallae. The whips were of coarse braided wool with the pastern bones of sheep knotted in, stained pinkish brown with old blood and new. The boy had been whispering something over and over between moans, but was obviously in that state where pain crosses back and forth over the line to pleasure. The whips fell again and again, leaving welts and cuts across the back, the shoulders, the curved buttocks. A beautiful boy, Jadviga thought, his own manhood growing hard and obtrusive under his tunic. He was not much for great burly men like himself, but boys were just as fine to take pleasure with as women. More, perhaps; they didn't grow big with child and demand you settle down and wed them.

The screaming frenzy of the gallae had reached a peak, as had the screaming of the crowd and the deafening noise of cymbals and drums. The boy was spinning now, frantically, naked under the whips. The other priestesses circled him, chanting. As the chant reached a peak, he was seized and thrown to his knees on the steps. A sharpened pottery shard was thrust into his hand, and his genitals were arranged on the step before him. Jadviga could not look away. The sacrifice of the Ing gods was done privately in a swamp by a priestess of Nerthus, not by one's own hand in front of the entire populace. The boy had raised his arm high, a strange ululating cry issuing from his throat. There was a collective indrawn breath, and then the hand fell with one sweeping motion.

The roar of the crowd was deafening. Oddly enough, the new galla did not scream, but only knelt gasping as if there was no sound left in her slender body. Blood splashed the temple steps, and the gallae fell to touch it and smear it on themselves. The newly emasculated youth tried to rise and failed, and instead held up the severed genitals in one hand and flung them into the crowd. There was an immediate scramble as twenty or thirty people hit the ground looking for the lost piece of flesh. Someone's mule brayed and bumped into Jadviga. He ignored it, watching the new galla's eyes roll up in her head as she fell. A half-dozen priestesses—real women, he noticed—who had been standing unmoved and away from the frenzy descended on her. A quill was inserted into the severed hole and hot, smoking pitch was smeared on the wound to stop the bleeding. She was bandaged with lightning quickness and borne away on a litter, and the last he saw of her was one hand trailing limply from the cloak thrown over her, a hand just a bit too large for a woman's, but much smaller than his own.

He had turned, then, wanting to get away from the riotous scrambling through the gutters near him, and then he noticed something at his feet. It was a tattered, fist-sized piece of flesh. One of the dogs was sniffing it, and growled at him as he bent to retrieve it. He had cuffed the cur, which had slunk off, and hid his new good-luck charm in his cloak as he had stolen out the other way.

Zagid tapped him on the shoulder, bringing him out of his memories with a jolt. His eyes were still fixed on her swaying ass, and his hand still clutched something that had once been a part of her flesh. He turned unseeing eyes to his employer. "Don't gawk, man," the Illyrian was saying, "unless you have gold coin to pay for your gawking. It's only polite to make offerings to the holy ones, and perhaps they'll tell your fortune. Me, I'll wait until the tax collectors have gone by."

The gallae went on down the road through the rubble of the city, and Jadviga tore his eyes from them and went back to heaving rock. His thoughts swirled like fish in a rainbarrel. I am mad, I am doomed, I must have her. I have carried her offering over my heart for nearly four years now. I must have the rest of her as well. But ... Baurux wants me to help with the ambush; he's got a backup of Thracian resisters and he needs my help. If I were to take her while the legion was here, the other gallae would make petition and I'd be in trouble. But if the soldiers were occupied by an ambush at the time ... Baurux, my friend, you'll have to go on this suicide mission without me.

Grunting, he heaved another stone into place and continued to plan his act of sacrilege.

■ ■ ■ ■

It was midnight, two nights later, that he crouched at the edge of a small field in the woods. Light from a flickering campfire shone through the open doorway of an abandoned barn. The Cybellines had chosen to sleep there until the houses were rebuilt and a celebration could be declared. The tax collector and his century had come through that morning; the village headman had wrung his hands and whined of how the bandits had taken everything, ruined the whole village, oh, it was terrible, everyone would probably starve this winter and his lordship must come back again next year, if anybody lived. He had handed over a few token coppers and been left untroubled.

Voices filtered through the doorway of the barn, feminine falsetto and masculine giggles. As he crept nearer, he could make out some of their conversation.

"—of course, that donkey's got to be replaced, girls. He's going to fall over any day now! Why, I swear he'll probably choose the middle of the procession to kiss the dust and die."

"And won't that be a poor omen, Glykera! Well, at least we did well enough in Salona that we can get a new one as soon as we find a town where the soldiers haven't bought all the extra mules for their wagons!"

"Aye, Delmatia's always fine this time of year. Fulvia! Pass that wine over here, dear. Aach! As bad as the stuff they give the legions, even!" There was a round of giggles and then one robed figure lurched out of the barn. Jadviga shrank back in the bushes. It was the tallest, ugliest one, apparently the leader, with a great mitred yellow cap on her bleached curls. "I must answer nature's call, my dears; wait until I get back before you swill all of that." She made her way, somewhat drunkenly, to the woods at the edge of the clearing.

It gave Jadviga an idea. The gallae were not unarmed; the larger ones had great antique axes and swords that they danced with in procession, but he expected that they knew how to use them. Apparently, feminine weakness went only so far with these "girls." Even his delicate little galla carried a large cupris knife at her belt. But where there was wine, there would be trips to the tree...

It was over an hour before she came out, a little drunk and a little wobbly, humming to herself. She had left her cupris behind. "Don't get lost, Philomena!" someone called after her, laughing. Jadviga cut around so as to be on her other side, upwind and out of the briars. She was humming to herself, her voice deeper than he expected. She lifted her skirts and squatted over an old tree stump; after her business was done she began to adjust her robes, and Jadviga got her from behind.

She was stronger than he had expected, too, and louder. She got two good squawks out before he managed to stuff enough moss in her mouth to shut her up, get her palla wrapped around to restrain her head and arms, fling her over his shoulder, and go. He had borrowed one of Baurux's two donkeys for the occasion; the bandit leader would not be happy but it couldn't be helped. There were sounds from the barn behind him, questioning calls. Jadviga got himself and his kicking bundle onto the donkey, lashed its tail with a bramble, and sped joltingly off into the night.

■ ■ ■ ■

Baurux's second cave was deserted, as he had expected. In case of defeat, they had stashed the lion's share of their raided wealth in this secondary stronghold, far from the cave in the crag where the Roman soldiers would pass below. He carried her to the farthest reaches, still struggling—she had scored a painful kick or two to his ribs—and dropped her to light more torches from the one feebly burning in its clay floor sconce. His sword, taken from a bandit he had quarreled with, was on his back; he unsheathed it and tore the palla from her head.

She was ready to jump and strike, but saw the tip of the blade just inches from her face and scrambled backwards instead. "By the Idumaean Mother, you are a cursed fool!" she hissed. "The death of a priestess of Cybele will not go unavenged, by the mortals or the gods!"

"I won't kill you," he said, feeling stupid. It had not occurred to him that she would assume her death. "I didn't bring you here to kill you."

"A barbarian!" She studied him, eyes narrowed. "Obviously you have never seen gallae before, and you mistook us for mere maidens. Let me go now, and I won't have you chopped into pieces."

Jadviga stared at her, letting his eyes linger on the curve of her throat, the feminine curls and the slight lump of her larynx. "I have seen you before," he said. "I know you. I want ... to know more of you." The sword tip wavered and lowered.

She stared at him. "You are mad!"

"Ja, I am mad. God-madness, this. Perhaps I have been touched by the pinecone of the Roman wine-god. He is a galla like you, is he not?" Jadviga grinned at her. The script for this scene had gone entirely by the wayside. He had no idea what to say, or do, to get what he wanted. Nor was he even sure what it was that he wanted, except to hold that slender body close and grunt out his pleasure in it. How do you tell a total stranger that you have been carrying them around in your heart for years, not to mention a mummified piece of their flesh?

"What do you want of me?" She was still suspicious, and frightened. He supposed he must seem very large to her.

"Your beauty." He squatted next to her and let the tip of the sword trace its way up her calf. She did not flinch or shrink away, only glared at him. "Your charm. Your grace. If I can have you for an hour, I will have it forever."

She snorted. "You want what all men want."

He laid down the sword—out of her reach—and extended a hand until it almost touched her face. "I am far from my home," he said softly, "and I may never return, and you are the only one in all these misbegotten lands that I have seen and wanted for more than an hour. The only one."

The galla shivered, almost hypnotized. "You ... you wanted me, more than a ... a woman who can bear children?" Her tone had changed completely, and there was silent pleading in it.

"What use are children to me, far from my home and people? Ja, it's you I want." Just for a second, he saw beyond her brave bluffing to the sheer courage it must have taken to become a creature that, although revered as holy, was not seen as truly a woman or a man. Who did not know what it was to be desired.

Her eyes dropped. "If I give you what you want, will you let me go?" There was almost a faint hope in her voice.

He considered it through the haze of his madness. Much as he wanted to chain her onto the back of that donkey and keep her with him forever, it was not a practical thing to hope for. "I will," he said haltingly.

She smiled. "My name is Philomena, barbarian. And I know what to do for your kind." She rolled over onto her belly and began to hike her skirt.

Jadviga ran a hand up the back of her leg, but she did not respond, being busy with her girdle. "No," he said suddenly. "This is not how I want it. If all I wanted was compliance, I could get it from any whore." He watched her practiced movements as she moistened between her buttocks with spit. You've done this too many times, haven't you, he spoke to her spirit. Spread yourself for an hour with men who did not care that you were wishing it was over, wishing it would never end. "Take off your clothes," he said.

She rolled back over and looked at him. "All of them? But it's cold."

"You'll be warm soon enough," he said thickly. Then he moved to the pile of discarded rubble and dirty dishes in the cave. Next to a brass cauldron still thick with grease from last night's dinner was a length of coarse tow rope. He turned back; her clothes were off, and she sat shivering on the stone floor, legs drawn up to hide herself.

Jadviga took her wrist in his large hand. Philomena resisted a moment when he began to tie the rope around it, but not enough to hurt herself. "I said I would give you what you wanted," she said in an annoyed tone. "Is my word not good enough?"

"Your word is fine," he said, securing both her wrists together and bringing her to her feet. "But your body is not speaking to me. You think I do not know its language, but you are wrong. I know you better than you think." He tied the rope to a tree root hanging down from the ceiling, cut off the rest of it, and secured her feet.

Philomena was turning pale. I have her, Jadviga thought grimly, undoing his broad leather girdle. "What do you think you know about me!" she whispered, never taking her eyes from his belt.

"I've seen enough of gallae to know where they get their real pleasure. And I saw you there, in Cyrene, on the Day of Blood." He lifted his arm in a familiar gesture and whipped the belt cruelly across her rounded buttocks.

She screamed. "You are mad!" she repeated, sobbing. He hit her again, and again. The red welts raised like plow tracks. Then, gently, he touched her between the tiny budded eunuch's breasts. This time her body responded to his hand with fervor, and she drew in her breath. "Please," she whispered. "This ecstasy is for the gods, not for you, barbarian."

Jadviga drew very close to her, stooping until his eyes were level with hers. "Tonight," he said, "I am your god." Then he seized her nipples in his fingers and squeezed them until she cried out, struggling in the bonds. Her body was plumper than it had been, but the waist was still narrow. He ran his hands over it, luxuriating in possessing her, but did not attempt to touch between her thighs.

Philomena was turning her face away from his, hiding in her long reddened hair. "Has no one touched you before?" he asked her in a whisper. "Has no one wanted you?" She did not answer, and it took a moment before he realized that he had spoken in Teutoni. "Let me give you what you save for the gods," he said in Latin, and resumed the beating. She twisted and screamed, louder and louder with each stroke on her back or buttocks, until suddenly she stopped abruptly as if her fear had been choked off. Startled, Jadviga looked at her face. Her eyes were wide open, staring, the pupils great and dark, and looking at nothing.

Then she began to mutter in a language he did not understand. Several languages. Some clear and bubbling, some rough and guttural. He recognized the iron tongue of the Saxons, High Gaulish and Low, Greek, Phoenician, and others, but could not make out a single word. Awed, he lifted his belt and let it fall, striping her chest in a crisscross pattern. The strange tongues babbled on and on, and she thrust out her thin chest in apparent pleasure. He went back to her buttocks, and she arched her back, body as tense as stone. The sounds trailed off to a low moaning, and then she gave one great shudder and cried out in what seemed to be a climax.

The belt slid out of his hand to the ground and he caught her as she sagged, hanging from the ropes. Jadviga pried at the knots around her wrists with his fingers, but she had pulled them too tight. He let go of her for a moment to pick up his sword and swung it in a clean arc, severing the rope, and then caught her again before she hit the ground. She clung to him, murmuring something in pidgin Latin, and he was suddenly, powerfully aroused.

Laying her gently down, he reached for the cauldron and got a handful of grease. Philomena was still only half in her body and did not resist as he spread her legs and smeared it into the crack of her ass. The flickering light showed the mass of scar tissue between her buttocks and the froth of her dark pubic hair. Jadviga had a queer throbbing sensation in his chest where the leather pouch lay inside his tunic, and he hesitated.

She opened her great dark eyes and looked at him. "Do you still want me?" she whispered.

"Ja," he gasped. "There's nothing I want more." And he found the right place between the cleft of her buttocks and slid into it. She wrapped her legs and arms around him and held him as he pumped himself deep inside her, burying her face in the blond pelt of his chest.

■ ■ ■

Afterwards, as she lay curled in his arms, he toyed with her fine silky hair and examined her just slightly overlarge hands in something like wonder. She shifted her position and looked up at him. "You've seen me before," she said. "Where did you say again?"

He stiffened in vague embarrassment. "Cyrene. I was in town on the Day of Blood. I saw you..." He trailed off.

She laughed, a little, and then touched his beard. "So you did. Did it shock you, barbarian, the glory of yielding to Cybele? Of course, I have always had bad luck, and the Day of Blood was no different. The tradition is that a new galla will be sheltered and fed, and given new clothes, by the family whose house her sacrifice is thrown into. But mine somehow disappeared, and I stayed in the temple, and was given the cast-off clothing of a sister that died."

Jadviga was taken aback. "I am sorry; I did not know," he said. He sounded so genuinely sorry that she looked at him from under her veil of hennaed hair.

"It is of no consequence," she said, and then donned a mischievous smile, as if it was a mask. "You make the beast with two backs well, for a barbarian," she said. "What is your name?"

"Jadvigus," he said, giving her the Latinized version. "And are we not beyond such whore's pretensions, you and I?"

She flushed, and sat up. "Since you will be off tomorrow, and I will not see you again, it makes no difference, does it not?"

He studied her, eyes narrowed, as she began to don her clothes. Her gestures were charmingly feminine. "Would you ever consider leaving the service of your goddess?"

"Never." Her tone was impassioned. "It is the only place I belong."

"There is no way I could change your mind, no way I could make you want to be mine?"

Philomena paused in the act of girding her chiton. She was silent and did not look at him, and something sparkled in her eye. "You already have some part of me, barbarian ... Jad-vigus. A part no mortal has touched before today."

"That," he said, "is probably true." And he pulled the small pouch from around his neck, undid the knots, and took out the desiccated offering, mummified with salt and Egyptian spices, and held it out to her.

She stared at it a long time, and then looked at him and then at it again, and then she screamed like a cat and launched herself at him. He was taken aback, and overbalanced. She beat on his chest with her not-so-small fists, cursing him, and then stopped, putting her hands on her hips and looking down at her surprised captor. "You," she said, leveling a finger at him, "owe me a new chiton, you bastard!"

"A new chiton," he repeated.

"And a palla. Green. And earrings of amber." At his expression, she burst out laughing.

■ ■ ■ ■

"And we were so worried, we roused half the men in the nearest house to look for you, and here you were off spreading yourself for this churl!" scolded Glykera. "You are lucky that the soldiers were off fighting bandits, or we would have had to send them to find you, little trollop!" In spite of the words, the tone was affectionate and the huge galla kept hiding a smile. Philomena had her mischievous grin on and would not let go of Jadviga's hand.

"But I have unfortunate news for your friend here," she went on. "This morning, the Romans came back with the heads of the bandit leaders, and they have decreed that all foreigners present themselves and state their reasons for traveling through the area. I do believe they are looking for Thracian spies."

Jadviga groaned. "Odin's wounds! I will have to try for the hills. Perhaps if I can find—"

Philomena laid a hand on his lips to quiet him and looked pleadingly at Glykera. "Could we ... perhaps ... tell the Romans that he is a servant of Cybele, with our temple?"

Jadviga sputtered and pushed away her hand. "I would rather be spitted on a Roman spear than be unmanned!" he protested.

Glykera laughed, dropping out of falsetto into a surprisingly hearty bass. "Foolish man! Not all who serve the temple are gallae. Someone has to take care of the donkeys."

"And this one is so big! Where did you find him, Philomena?" cooed Fulvia, batting her heavily kohled lashes. "Perhaps if we save him from the Romans, he'll be ... properly grateful."

"Come, dear." Philomena tucked her arm into his and drew him inexorably along towards the town. "We'll take care of everything. None of the villagers will gainsay us; after all, we're sacred. And as for the Romans, well, we're the official representatives of one of the official temples of the Palatine hill. After they've gone, and the rebuilding is done, we've got a festival to attend to. You wouldn't want to miss that, would you? Especially since there are bound to be peddlers and you still owe me something."

"Odin's wounds and Freya's ass," Jadviga muttered, eyeing the flock of gallae who were clustering around him like oversized fluttering birds, openly flirting. "Ah well, I suppose there's no choice." As he moved off with Philomena, he remembered the advice his father had given him. Be careful what you ask for.

He decided not to finish the sentence in his head.

HISTORICAL NOTES

In the Roman era, the temple of Cybele was a haven for individuals we would today consider transsexuals. Self-castrated, they lived as women and priestesses, and were one of the more popular faiths of the area. Cybele was originally an Asiatic goddess from what is now modern-day Turkey. Although the common folk greatly respected the gallae, intellectual upper-class Romans were horrified and disgusted by them and passed a law stating that anyone who so mutilated his genitalia could not be a Roman citizen. The word "galla" is the feminized form of the Latin word for rooster, a Roman play on words.

The gallae were fascinated with the use of flagellation and cuttings in order to achieve religious trance. Their festivals always included some form of flagellation—of themselves, of each other, of anyone who offered themselves to the whips. While "on tour," they would flog and cut themselves with knives and swords until they were in altered states and the crowds would shower them with money for their pain.

Many of the trappings of the Cybelline temple were adopted by the Catholic Church. The robe and mitre of bishops and popes is copied directly from the ceremonial costume of archigallae.

In the North, the godhi seidhr-kraefter, while similar in custom to the Cybellines in their use of transgendered priests, were part of a secret society and their rites were not open to the public.

This story would have taken place around A.D. 160 in the area we now know as Albania.

Anyone interested in the gallae or other ancient practices of religious SM or transgenderism is encouraged to contact the author through the publisher.

WILHELM'S CONCESSION

"Yasmin. You know better than that."

It was the frown more than the disapproving hiss that made her stop and put aside the tray. Wilhelm Schmidt had always had a handsome face, at least for a white man. She much preferred to see that face happy. Smiling, contented.

It took her back to 1915 all over again.

As if by magic.

Yasmin firmly planted her bare feet in the dirt and brought herself up straight. She put her shoulders back, so her arms thrust down her sides and her rubbery, near-purple nipples stood out with pride.

Perhaps it was a blasphemy to equate mere memories of her past with the Visions. With the bright and terrible images of the future. With the power that took her, made her an Instrument of Eternity at the very moment of fulfillment.

Perhaps.

But she was already a traitor. To her people. To her father and all the others, the long and noble line of Shamans and Gifted Ones from which she descended.

She had allowed herself to love a white man. A very young and strangely innocent white man. One whose people had temporarily put aside their own bloodstained dispute with the English to join them. English and German both, united to crush John Chilembwe's dream.

And Yasmin, willful and no older than the century, welcoming the boyish white man's touch. His urgent kisses. His pale, lunging shaft and spurting seed.

So Yasmin was a traitor. Had been now, for more years than not. A traitor.

And a Gifted One. Untrained in the Mystic Arts. Who saw Visions only when she and her pale, foreign consort drove each other to unspeakable, unholy ecstasies. When they played The Game.

Was it really worse—or even surprising—that she should also, eventually, turn blasphemer?

Yasmin shivered, despite the building heat and humidity of a late-March afternoon. Wilhelm saw and wondered, but did not ask.

The Game had its rules. At this point, compassion was not to be shown. Nor tenderness, nor concern. And most certainly, not respect.

She faced him directly, eyes unblinking and chin elevated in silent protest. Her dark, angular face was set. Her serene challenge wordlessly proclaimed that she was more than a Servant.

And far more than an erotic implement; more than a living sex toy for Wilhelm Schmidt to use or lend out as he saw fit.

He shook his head to escape the bondage of their locked, throbbing gazes. He stepped abruptly to her, resolved that she must not see what anticipation had already done to his crotch. He stared at the bare, ebony orbs mounted high upon her chest.

Defiance must be answered. That was the rule and the reality that the two of them had worked out together. It fit perfectly with the time and place in which they found themselves. And with the invariable expectations of outsiders, black and white alike.

Her milk-glands felt warm and spongy to his slow-flexing, widely deployed fingers. They were slick with her steady, constant perspiration. Though she pleaded with herself, her nipples hardened to beads against his pressing palms.

To become aroused by his touch, even when she knew what awaited her—that was a fitting, humiliating way for it to begin.

Now Wilhelm brought the narrow gap of his mouth to her lush, undecorated lips. Yasmin hated herself for wanting that kiss. But she did want it, desperately.

Of course he sensed that. Of course he halted, no more than a millimeter short of a passionately oral union. He lingered there, so close that any time one of them spoke their soft flesh brushed together. Taunting, torturing them both.

But especially the needy, presently submissive Yasmin.

His right hand shifted. He pinched, twisted her nipple until she winced. Forcing a grin, Wilhelm slid both hands down her exposed torso. He made the contact as lewd as possible and halted only when he reached the rounded prominence of her hip. He undid the light skirt and let it slither from his fingertips down her legs.

One hand went between her legs. He rubbed her folds, squeezed and rubbed again. Yasmin gasped and averted her eyes, again ready to follow orders.

She responded to his sharp whisper, stepped free of the discarded garment. Now she was nude, except for the long, colorful, scarf-like cloth about her head and the massive, hand-carved ivory earrings that sagged down to brush against the tops of her shoulders.

"Now," he told her in the deceptively quiet German he had made her fluent in. "You are ready to serve my guest. Yes?"

Her eyes flickered up. "Ready to serve you, Master."

The slap followed instantly and loud, but not especially hard. Still, Yasmin's face tingled excitedly. Her eyes fell and she murmured compliance. She carefully kept the sound of pleasure from her voice.

Wilhelm resumed with his hand cupped over her deep furrow. He collected, spread her aromatic outflow. They could both smell her readiness now. The new Government man, Pender, would also be able to, Yasmin reflected.

Shame and anticipation made her musky juice flow only stronger.

At last his hand pulled back from her crotch. His other hand gestured and Yasmin folded to her knees. Her face a perfect blank, she licked her fluids from his palm, his fingers. Then she flattened her hands to either side of him on the dirt floor and leaned over, to play her broad tongue across the faintly muddy upper regions of his boots.

Unseen by her, Wilhelm let his stolid expression soften. He looked down at her with regret and love. If only there was another way to ensure his position!

But it served The Game. That, at least, gave both of them pleasure.

Yasmin paused, but did not look up. She murmured, rubbed her wide nose against his instep as she spoke. "And of tonight, Master?" Her eyes closed tight as she waited for his reply.

"If you behave properly, you may have some slight reward." It was as close to a promise as The Game allowed.

Yasmin's head remained down as Wilhelm turned, made his exit. Then she rose, took the opportunity to prepare herself.

The men were slumped comfortably back in the wicker chairs, basking in the sunshine across the low table from each other. Yasmin, the tray and its open bottle, its pair of tall glasses balanced expertly on her hip, came swaying provocatively past Pender's lazy, dangling arm. Her naked crotch was level with the man's mouth as she served the wine, her labial folds open like a blossoming flower.

Reginald Pender stared, astonished to discover the whispers he'd heard were true. His new posting, as Special Assistant to the Royal Governor for Land Use Policy, had some truly remarkable perks. Especially here, in the isolated and clearly uncivilized interior!

Pender's saggy face worked as he slurped his drink and waited for Concessionaire Schmidt to acknowledge his interest. It wouldn't do for him to simply reach for the bitch and take her, in front of her Master and without invitation.

Yasmin and Wilhelm both read his expression instantly. She held back her disgust and turned, bent slightly forward and took her time filling Wilhelm's glass. This gave the stranger time to enjoy her plump, round ass and the even more profound blackness of the canyon between the perfectly matched globes.

It was Wilhelm's place to actually respond. His Concession, his exclusive right to graze cattle on the surrounding land might be at stake. Yet again. The document dated from his father's time, from before the World War. When Tanganyika had been the centerpiece of German East Africa and not merely one of many, many British possessions.

The Concession had been extended, on certain conditions. The high and mighty English did not easily grant special privileges to foreigners. His service against the Native uprising in Nyasaland had helped. But other actions, formal and otherwise, had been required of him in the eighteen years since.

Now, again, he was faced with the most informal of them all. He told himself it was necessary. For her, as much as for himself. He told himself that The Game was what mattered. And this would further it; this was a key and vital part of it.

Wilhelm ceased his discussion of Herr Hitler and the "temporary" powers Hitler had just been given over Germany. In any case, Pender did not take the man at all seriously. The British idiot laughed to remember the beer-hall rebellion the same man had tried back in '23. Now, a decade later, such an international joke was to make Germany run?

"He may indeed be a lunatic," Wilhelm had tried to tell Pender. "But he's a dangerous one. He'll lead Germany to total ruin!"

"So it's just as well you renounced citizenship, huh?"

Outraged, Wilhelm had nearly blurted out the bits and pieces that he knew. That he and Yasmin had pieced together, matching her stark Visions to the wireless broadcasts, the foolishly hopeful articles in the outdated newspapers they received sporadically.

"What makes you think," he finally asked, "that Hitler might not take your precious England down with him, too?"

Pender had blinked at that. And shook his head, refusing to believe anyone—even a chap as off as Hitler—would be crazy enough to plunge them all into a second world war.

Then Yasmin had come into view and Pender had lost what interest he had in the distant obscurities of European politics.

Yasmin felt this new man's leer glide over her ass and she gave Wilhelm a slow look that asked sardonically if he was happy and dared him to follow through with it.

Your guest is waiting, Herr Schmidt. Waiting for his warm, wet, fleshy bribe.

Pender raised his empty glass, cleared his throat and cocked a sloppy eyebrow.

Wilhelm nodded, gestured.

Yasmin turned. Her breasts wobbled, dangling as she bent across the table to refill Pender's glass. He moaned, his attention focused on her long, dark nipples. His hand slipped and wine slurped over the rim of his glass, spattering the tabletop.

With smirking unconcern, Wilhelm waved off Pender's apology and told him to relax. "Yasmin will clean it up. It's her job, you understand." And then he gave the woman's bare rump a loud, playful, open-handed slap.

Her face a perfect blank, Yasmin put aside the tray and the wine bottle. The glasses, too, as soon as the men had them drained. Then, returning to Wilhelm's elbow, she placed her fingertips along the table's edge and bent forward at the waist. She stared with wide eyes up at Pender and her tongue unfurled. Yasmin lapped the wine from the wooden surface in a series of slow, sensual, arcing passes.

The table was so low that Pender's belted crotch was actually several inches above it and in plain view. The English bureaucrat was hard, uncomfortably so. He let out a faint groan as Yasmin finished.

Fingering her asshole casually, Wilhelm rose and took a new position, directly behind Yasmin. "My guest is in discomfort, Yasmin. Be a good little black girl and help him. Help him now!" He punctuated the last word with a flailing, double-palmed blow that made her buttocks wobble and Yasmin's whole body jump.

Her expression still absolutely neutral, Yasmin extended herself across the table. She undid Pender's belt, opened his khaki shorts and began to lick the cap of his erection. His dick was thick but not too long. It grew another inch or so in her pumping fist—a hairy pink shaft in the grip of supple ebony.

Pender started to leak precum out on her tongue and she dipped her head, smeared the pearly outflow in thin streamers across her cheeks and nose. Then she tucked him into her mouth and inhaled his full length effortlessly. Her lips tightened and relaxed about the Englishman's base in rhythm with the slow thrusts Wilhelm was using, directing a pair of fingers in and out of her bubbling vagina.

At the exact right moment, Wilhelm reached with the other hand and yanked the headwrap off, revealing Yasmin's smooth and hairless skull.

Every morning for eighteen years now, she had shaved his face for him and he had returned the favor with her head. They both were quite good at it, by now.

Pender gasped louder than ever. He slapped both hands down on the back of her slowly rotating skull. They clawed at her, then began to move. To search for firm purchase on the smooth, sweaty curve of her head.

One fist took her jaw; the other snagged an ear, nearly dislodged one of Wilhelm's most extravagant tokens of love. Pender tensed, held her motionless and lunged, climaxing in her mouth. She closed her eyes, drank as much as she could before gagging.

Yasmin's head bucked free, semen cascading down her chin. She let him hold his dick against her, till the last of his discharge finished oozing out upon her face.

Then Yasmin moved partway around the table and knelt. She passively followed her white Master's orders and flattened herself on the tabletop. Exchanging grins and rude murmurs, the two men took turns fucking her from behind. Pender used her asshole as well as her pussy.

Through it all, Yasmin was silent.

Accepting.

As if it was all completely natural.

Pender laughed and slapped his knuckles against Wilhelm's chest as he tucked his exhausted dick back in his shorts with the other hand. "I don't think we've any irregularities with your Concession, Mr. Schmidt. Or should I say Herr Schmidt?"

Wilhelm shrugged, walked the official to his battered Royal Government touring car. Pender drove off whistling, just ahead of the evening showers.

Her face still marked with streaks of drying man-juice, Yasmin drank wine from the bottle as Wilhelm shuttered the house against the driving rainstorm. Then he came to her, methodically shed his clothing and lowered his head in sensually compelling shame.

"Time for me to serve you, Mistress."

Yasmin grinned, moved her legs farther apart, and took a long, deep gulp of wine. He was on his knees, light fingertips parting her and his tongue darting in from below, even before she finished swallowing. He ate her with submissive loyalty and skill, nibbling and gumming her folds. Then he crawled, wriggling like a pale worm between her legs. He came up behind to suckle adoringly at her anus.

"Go into the bedroom," she ordered. "I will join you, when I feel like it."

She did, once she had selected what she wanted from a bulging steamer trunk.

Wilhelm turned eagerly onto his knees and raised his bare ass upon sighting the swagger stick. The bristled hyena's tail on the end added a weird teasing quality as Yasmin paddled his ass, snarling at him in Chichewa. Like her, he had learned her native tongue. Now, he nodded and moaned back at her, agreeing that indeed he was a low thing, from a lower-than-low people. A people they both knew would soon bring even worse horrors to an already horrible world.

He accepted it all, with moaning willingness. And when she strapped herself into the long, tapering ivory dildo, he welcomed it. Every stroke was like a cleansing, opening his asshole to let the guilt flow out.

She reached around him, her body molded to his back. Yasmin milked the semen from him with both hands, and the sheer excitement set her off as well. The sacred dildo was like a connecting rod between them, completing a supernatural circuit far more potent than anything merely electric.

They shared the rush of images behind their tightly closed, tearing eyes. Her Visions became his. Became Theirs.

And they went much further, were more coherent than before.

At last, they saw past the blood and hate. Past savagery the rest of the world could hardly begin to imagine. A thing so subtle and slow, humanity could hardly credit its existence even centuries beyond them. But a real thing, and one that would, eventually, remake the worlds of humankind.

The Vision faded.

Yasmin eased her dildo from Wilhelm's ass. They undid the straps and kissed. On their sides, rubbing noses and caressing, they joined once more. Murmuring words of love in German, Chichewa, English, and even the local dialect of Swahili, they made slow love deep into the night.

The Game would be played again, many times. Sometimes ruthlessly; sometimes with laughter. Sometimes he would lead; sometimes she. But never again—no matter what the world outside might say or think or threaten— never again would it be played with anything but hope.

THE BRIDE'S STORY

"Eeee!"

"Von! It's Von!"

Blue and yellow knee-length dresses flouncing, six Demish girls jumped up and down trying to get a glimpse of their visitor.

"Girls!" Matron drove them away from the door, radiating disapproval. The girls would see him soon enough at the bride's party. On the eve of her arranged marriage, a Demish bride celebrated with her peers. Matron still remembered the games and the beautiful, highly skilled courtesans who came to perform for her, but in her day, the courtesans were all female. Today, seventeen-year-old Princess Lillan would spend her bride's party with five girl cousins and one male courtesan, Von. The girls' pale cheeks were flushed with excitement and Matron waved a hand at them. "Back in you go now! I must have a word with him."

Von was a rising star with the old women of the court and Matron knew it well. She considered it a dangerous vogue that the girls now demanded their favorites from rumors told by servants and loose-lipped older relatives. She herself was ninety years old, but like most Demish widows in the long, stable stretch of Sevolite adulthood she had avoided commoner-style aging. She looked to be a well-worn but healthy thirty. Despite her resilient physique, Matron did not enjoy her extended youth with the abandon of her aunts and sisters. She disliked men—particularly courtesans. At least the pompous selfishness of Demish men was honest.

Matron shoved at the little one trying to peek around her legs. "Ow!" the child objected.

"Lillan!"

"Come on." Princess Lillan reluctantly reclaimed command of her party guests. "Matron won't eat him. He'll still be there to look at in five minutes."

"But—"

"We've already waited—"

"Is he pretty? I've never seen a man that's pretty. Will he look like a girl, then?"

"Hush!" When she had her younger cousins in control, Lillan made to join Matron in delivering Von's instructions, but Matron turned her away with a frown, leaving her as vexed with the delay as all the others.

In the hall, Von cocked a thin eyebrow at Matron from the shadows of his hooded cloak.

"Come," she barked, and marched him into an anteroom across the foyer. Matron eyed the courtesan as he stood just inside the door, a lithe shape draped in soft black folds, out of place among the embroidered throws and racks of porcelain ladies in a constellation of sedate positions.

"Let me see you," she ordered.

Von shed his traveling cloak. His off-white tunic and lounge pants looked touchably soft, the tunic sporting a loose fold across the chest, trimmed in gold, with a braided belt of the same pliant material. He was barefoot, his shoes with the house porter, where they were left on his arrival.

"You come with good references," allowed Matron. "You've performed at other children's parties without incident. But I've heard the gabbing of those satisfied clients with which I am, unavoidably, acquainted." With practiced control, Matron allowed the politeness of her voice to show her distaste. "These girls are innocents. The men expect them to be that way, and demand its blessing until marriage is forced upon them. So do not imagine you know what is expected here because you have been in the beds of their bored aunts and grandmothers. The only men they've much to do with at all are frightened servants and foreboding uncles. Do you understand what I am saying?"

"I think so, Your Grace."

She frowned as if at something slimy. His intelligent understanding had the air of a gift about it, which she heartily resented for a parlor trick. "What is it you specialize in?"

"Sword dancing."

"Too provocative. Do you sing?"

"Yes."

"Tell stories?"

He nodded.

"Stick to things of that nature." She gave him another once-over. His hair was jet, his lips pastel, his features finer than those of her porcelain maidens. Add to that a dancer's grace and strength, and eyes like cut gems of gray crystal. He was dangerous. A carefully tutored false advertisement, an icon for an adult society Lillan and the rest did not know the truth of.

"Remember," she warned, frowning. "Be careful."

She led him back to the children waiting in the room bedecked for the party. They were dancing in a circle. When the door opened they dropped hands and swarmed around him.

"This is Von, of Den Eva's," announced Matron. "Von, this is tomorrow's bride, Princess Lillan."

The girls fell silent. Matron watched them stare at him like a piece of breathing sculpture, his beauty worn with a studied carelessness.

Lillan curtsied and Von raised her gently. "You mustn't do that, Your Highness. I'm commoner."

Lillan was wide-eyed. "But you're so beautiful."

As beautiful as the romantic prince-hero from a court ballad, Matron thought and shook her head. These girls' real lives would be far removed from that. Simsa was shy; she would be her husband's willing decoration. Danda was insipid. Both of them would take up with courtesans in their middle years because their peers were doing it. Fifteen-year-old Vrassa would be one of the trendsetters. She and fourteen-year-old Ola were already competing. When they were older, they would try to outdo one another's wickedness. Tala, at eleven, was all bounce and boldness and too young to predict. But Lillan she felt the most sorry for. Lillan the romantic.

Von was smiling at them all. "Thank you for having me to entertain you. What shall we start with?"

"Dance, please?" Tala begged. "I want to see sword dances!"

Matron watched his answer carefully as he flicked a glance toward her. "Oh," said Von, "to sword dance I would need a trained partner. Besides, I would rather learn your dances. Can you teach me?"

The girls eagerly dragged him to the center of the room and began a round of dancing tag. They circled and circled until the ring broke in a mad scramble.

"One—two—three—four! You lose!" cried Tala, as each girl tagged the unprepared Von.

"Oh, so that is how you play this game," said Von. "Let us have another round."

And so they did, the girls petting him like a tame dog. A flush, a touch, too much body contact...

By the fifth round, the girls piled upon him.

Matron rose, clapping her hands to be heard over the shrieks of laughter. "Lori!" She summoned the serving girl to divert them. "Refreshments!"

Lori hurried in with a tray, long legs scissoring and dishwater-dull eyes downcast.

Von evaded Vrassa's efforts to help him straighten his clothing.

"Tell us a story," begged Lillan.

"That's a good idea," Matron said, glad of a change from such physical games. "Something quiet."

Lillan took Von's hand. "Tell us the story of Princess Demora."

"That's mushy!" Ola objected.

"It's about love," Von allowed, catching Ola's hand to draw her toward Lillan. "Demora began much like Lillan," he began, "a girl obliged to marry by contract. But, she already loved another." He placed Ola's hand in Lillan's, casting them as hero and heroine. As he recited the story, he cast each of the other children into the roles of Demora's in-laws and others. They listened spellbound as he directed them with the magic of the story and gestures. Lori's platter went unnoticed by everyone except Matron, who eyed the sliced fruit and wafers with annoyance.

There were tears in bright blue eyes when the hero received his mortal wound, redeeming Demora from the false accusations of her in-laws. Ola lay on the floor with her head in Lillan's lap as Vrassa, in the part of the husband, stood by frowning and Tala, playing the physician, looked up to pronounce with Von, "The wound is mortal."

Lillan sobbed aloud.

"That's enough," Matron said, and stood over the troop on the floor. "Clear the things, Lori. The party is over."

Von broke off, blinking, as if jarred himself to be robbed of the story's sentimental ending. Simsa, Danda, Ola, and Lillan flocked around Matron, whimpering their protest.

"Can't we finish?"

"He's only been here an hour!"

"It's so sad ... Poor Demora."

"Such nonsense!" pronounced Matron.

A movement caught her eye. It was Vrassa. Matron parted the crowd of skirts and golden locks around her in time to see, but not stop, the girl from throwing herself at Von with vigor.

She'd caught him off guard as he stooped to gather up some props they'd been using in the drama. He fell over, with her on top of him.

She shamelessly kissed him on the mouth.

Danda screamed in alarm. "You'll get pregnant!"

Von began to disengage himself from Vrassa. Tala made as if to help him up. Matron crossed the room in two strides, and caught Tala by one hand even as her other slipped between his parted thighs. "Tala!"

"It's soft," the child said, sitting back on her knees, unrepentant. "How could he stick it through you?"

Von chuckled. Matron stiffened. He stifled the chuckle and said in a soft voice, "No one gets wounded."

"Oh, Tala," Lillan apologized in a fluster. "How awful. She's so brazen."

"What *does* happen?" Vrassa demanded.

"I thought *you* knew!" Ola remarked.

Tala pulled her hand free of Matron. "Tell us?"

Matron never expected what happened next. After all her warnings to him, Von had the audacity to answer. "Don't do what you don't enjoy. Enjoy all that you're able to. That's the best I—"

"On your feet!" Matron snapped, pushing Danda away from her.

Von stood and the girls peeled away from him.

"Lillan," Matron ordered. "Say goodbye to your guests, and call their escorts. Then come see me. We've things to discuss before your wedding."

"Matron's going to tell *her*," complained Ola.

"Shh." Lillan started to herd them off. She paused to glance over her shoulder. "Goodbye, Von. And thank you. It was a great party."

Matron saw the wan smile on his lips. No doubt he realized he was in trouble.

"We will take this up in private," she told him. "Lori! You will come also."

"But I didn't—"

"I did not say you did anything, girl. Just do as you are told."

Matron hurried them down the hall to her apartment. They passed through her office, into the lounge, then the private dining room. She opened the bedroom door. Dark hints of the polished wood and russet reds of the furnishings showed through the doorway, formal and foreboding.

Von stood still. Matron held the door wide for both of them. Von's left hand flexed. Lori was fidgeting. "Inside," Matron told them both, impatient. Lori darted in with a little moan. Von obeyed silently.

Matron pulled the door closed, then paused with it open a mere crack. The two of them were talking. What could this courtesan have to say? She listened while she waited for Lillan to join them.

Von voice was soft as he said, "You'd better calm down."

"I—I—"

She heard water being poured from the pitcher beside her bed. "Drink this. You'll feel better."

"It's different for you," Lori blurted. "People want you. You have talent. There's nowhere to go if I'm thrown out! I'd just starve. I'm nobody."

"I've met worse people," he answered with kindness. Was he trying to seduce the girl? Matron wondered.

Lori sniffed. "How can you be so calm?"

"I'm not. I'm a good actor."

Lillan arrived, still wearing her frilly party dress. Matron took her hand. "Come with me, dear."

Von was sitting on the chest at the end of Matron's bed. He sprang up. Lori put her water glass down guiltily. Lillan look at Matron in surprise. "I thought we were going to talk about men," she said, clutching Matron's hand harder.

"We are dear," said Matron. "Von, stand up on that chest."

It was one easy step. He faced Matron, his waist now at eye level. The bed's russet canopy brushed his head.

"On my wedding night," Matron told Lillan, "I had absolutely no idea what a man was. You will." She untied Von's belt.

Lillan pressed a fist to her mouth. "What are you doing?"

"He's a courtesan," Matron said blandly. "He does what he's paid for."

"Don't!" Lillan caught Matron's hands as she started to jerk Von's breeches down.

"Very well, then," said Matron. "You do it."

Lillan bit her lip. The soft cloth of Von's tunic moved with each breath he took. She put her hand on it. She held her breath. Matron watched her eyes travel up, and frowned, but Von avoided eye contact. He was looking across the room.

"At first, men struck me as ugly," Matron informed her, guiding her hand lower. "Then ridiculously vulnerable." Lillan resisted and she released her. "Take your clothes off," she instructed Von. "All of them."

Lori turned her head with a tiny gasp.

Von stripped off his soft tunic.

"Oh!" sighed Lillan.

"You can see as much on any statue in a public corridor," Matron reminded him. "It's their tender spots men keep to themselves, so they can frighten you with them. She jerked down Von's breeches. He flinched slightly.

Lillan's lips parted. She stepped back and stared. "What ... is it?"

Matron sorted out organs through Von's fine mesh of pubic hair. At her rude touch, Von braced himself with a hand on either post of the single bed. "These are testicles. They're tender. You can disable a man if you hurt him here." Von obliged her with a muffled sound as she gave an experimental squeeze. He closed his eyes.

"This is what gets rigid," Matron continued her inventory. "He can't do it at will, but you can make it stiff easily with handling. It's what they put inside you."

Horror showed on Lillan's face. "But—where!"

"Lori!"

"May I dress?" Von asked quietly.

"No. Come down here." Matron pulled Lori toward him as he stepped off the wooden chest. "Demonstrate," she ordered him, "on the servant girl."

"No!" Lori tried to escape. Matron caught her by the arm. "Don't be a silly girl. There are princesses who pay a great deal for this."

"I don't think I can, Your Grace," Von demurred.

"Don't be silly. By all reports you are as tireless as royalty."

"It's not that—it's—if you could find someone willing? I mean the girl."

Matron squeezed Lori's arm. "You're willing, aren't you?"

"Yes, Matron," she whimpered.

"There." Matron thrust her at the naked man.

Von gathered her against his chest, her tears and runny nose wet on his skin. "Have you done this before?" he asked. She shook her head from side to side. "It might hurt," he said, "but it will be worse if you are tense and frightened."

Her voice climbed toward a wail. "I can't help it!"

He kissed her on the edge of her lips. "Pretend that you're dreaming," he whispered and she clung to him. "You will not get pregnant," he promised. She nodded against his chest and he rubbed the back of her neck.

Matron decided this was taking too long. "Do it on the floor. There's no need to soil the bed."

Lillan was surprised again. "Does it make a mess?"

Von eased Lori onto the carpet.

"Too slow and too gentle," Matron hissed. "It won't be like that for Lillan tomorrow."

But Von loosened Lori clothing, advising her to touch him as he massaged some flexibility into her rigid limbs. "Like this, it helps." She stared up at him, hanging onto his advice and terrified of him all at once. He kissed her, using only his lips. She relaxed slightly, only to grow brittle as his hand moved up her thigh.

"You see that?' Matron pointed to Von's stiffening member.

"Is it really hard like a sword?" Lillan wondered.

"Touch it."

She looked at Matron and Matron urged her with her eyes. Lillan slipped down to the floor and reached out her hand toward Von. Von was wise enough to help. No sooner did she touch him than she snatched back her hand and scrambled away, proud of her courage but half upset.

Lori had curled up into a ball. Von began coaxing her open once again.

"Do it fast," Matron ordered. "She must know what it's going to be like for her. The first time is the worst. But, like childbirth, it would be easier if she knew what to expect."

He took a deep breath. For a moment, Matron thought he was going to resist, though she couldn't imagine why. This could hardly be difficult work for him. Finally, he took Lori's shoulders and forced her to lie back. He used his knee to separate hers. She began to pant with fear.

Von rocked back, a hand fisted near his waist.

"What's the matter?" Matron folded her arms in exasperation.

"I can't!"

"You look perfectly capable," she said, noting the state of his organs. Why would a courtesan be so reluctant? She thought she had it. "Of course, you will be paid extra."

"No." He looked her in the eye. "I can't do it."

Matron matched his stare, expecting his to break. But his jaw was white with anger and other emotions. "You'd both be ill advised to spoil this lesson," she said coldly.

"I'm willing!" Lori bleated. "I really am willing, please!"

Von gave the servant girl a hot, resentful look. "You're slightly more willing than you are to starve to death!" He was losing his erection and closed his eyes briefly. When he opened them, he concentrated on Lillan, using a sweeter voice. "Perhaps there are things I could tell you, or show you, without—"

"Lori!" Matron pointed to the chest. "There's an old sword in that chest. Get it out, in its sheath." The sword had belonged to Matron's father and would be a suitable instrument. "And you, Von, lie across the top of this chest. Let her sheath-whip you, if you'd prefer that to doing what you are asked for reasonable compensation! You *are* a good actor. But I am not as easily manipulated as a crowd of virgin girls. We will do this on my terms."

Lori stood hugging the jewel-studded saber in its heavy, velvet-covered sheath, inhaling with little, sharp hiccups and staring like a mad woman. Von's stare, though, looked sullen. Matron ordered, "Get on the chest."

He balked. Lillan interrupted. "Oh no, Matron!"

"He's just playing a role to raise the price," said Matron. "He'll change his mind before he'll take a beating."

"He's protecting poor Lori!" Lillan countered.

"A sentimental courtesan? Lillan, you have much to learn. Hit him where he stands!"

Lori swung wildly. Von evaded the blow easily, snapping out his hand to grab the sheath. Lori pulled back and drew the sword. They faced one another, Von with the sheath and Lori with the naked blade. Lori looked as though she might drop the blade. Matron snatched it away from her and slapped at Von's head with the flat of it. He parried with the sheath. "Drop that!" she railed at him. How dare he fight back! Here, where she had all the power!

Her rage shocked and frightened him. He held out the sheath. "Don't use the sword," he said. "You'll kill me." She jerked the sheath from his hand and struck. He had no rights here! He would not turn the tables and make her the villain. This was for Lillan.

He defended his head with his naked arm and she beat him across the back. He went down and she struck again, the metal tip of the sheath raising a welt that began to bleed.

"Stop it!" Lillan grappled with her, shrieking. "Stop!"

Matron dropped her bludgeon and caught Lillan's arms. "You don't—understand—" she gasped, trying to make Lillan see that her horror was misplaced. "Husbands ... are animals. Courtesans are paid. That's all there is. Just lies! No heroes."

"He wouldn't hurt her, and you beat him because he wouldn't hurt her!"

Matron sighed. Lillan still did not understand. "Lillan—"

"It was *nice* of him! It was brave! Even if he's just a commoner!" The young princess tore away in an explosion of tears and fled noisily, the door slamming shut behind her.

Matron swayed. Where had the lesson gone wrong? Von straightened up, on his knees, and Lori blubbered. Matron spoke numbly. "You may leave, Lori. There's a good girl."

Lori gave a sob and, following Lillan, ran from the room and slammed the door.

Matron sat down in a carved upholstered chair.

After a long, quiet minute, Von asked, in a small voice, "Can I get dressed?"

"Stand up."

He made a throaty noise as he climbed to his feet, less graceful than before but with no sign of crippling injury.

There were marks coming up in welts, and there would be bruises. Matron snatched a dressing gown from the chair and hurled it at him. He caught it, but did not put it on.

"Why wouldn't you do it?"

He did not answer.

"Tell me!"

He drew the gown around his shoulders, dragging it through the ooze of blood on his back. His left hand gripped his right forearm. The rest of his stance slowly relaxed, but he seemed to have lost his voice.

"I could put it about that you molested Tala," Matron said. "You'd never work near Demish girls or their mothers again."

He looked up at last. "Don't!"

"Then, tell me. And make it convincing."

"I've ... been raped."

She let out the breath she had been holding. There was a long silence while he forced himself to inhale and struggled with his composure

"Come here," she said. He approached, without limping, and stopped within easy reach of her if she leaned forward.

"Look at me."

She watched as he struggled to keep his feelings off his face.

"How old were you?"

He swallowed. He tried to speak, but started to shiver and paused to gain control of that first before he began again, eyes focused past her. "I ... don't know. A child."

"By a man?"

He nodded.

"Often"

"I see." She waited out another minute of silence. "I was a child myself."

His gray eyes lifted, surprise and compassion in them.

"A child bride," said Matron, "like Lillan."

He knelt down in front of her, sinking like a sigh despite his bruises. His eyes stayed with hers.

"I try to prepare my girls," she told him. "I try to ready them, so they won't face it without weapons. Knowledge. Hatred to help them through it. It's cruel help at best."

"You are not wrong," he said, his voice offering gifts of understanding. "I have heard about Demish husbands. And I am paid." He touched her knee, lightly.

She took his hand. His fingers were long and clever, a smear of blood on his palm. She rubbed the blood away with her thumb and set his hand onto her knee again, holding it quiet, beneath her own.

"Would you like me to talk with Lillan?" He spoke as if they had known each other a long time and shared this problem.

"Yes." Matron let his hand slide free and immediately missed its warmth and pliant strength. In his eyes shone the promise to learn, to teach, and to keep the results private. He rose to dress.

"And come again," she said, in a rush, as he made his way to the door.

"For the next bride's lesson?"

"For the bride of long ago, who missed her lesson."

He smiled freely at her then. "I can do that, yes."

GONAR'S SAGA

n the cool hours before dawn Gonar stretched his big muscles and smiled to himself, thinking of the ruby firestone. He had never seen anything like it: a disc the width of his palm that could focus the sun's rays to ignite kindling. It would be splendid suspended from a gold chain, hanging like an amulet on his bronzed chest, the most beautiful jewel in Jhent. Even King Rhanges would envy him!

The newcomer, Chom, probably thought he had some secret technique for winning the wager, but Gonar had seen and felt everything that Shegri had to offer. The rules of the contest were in his favor. There could be no scars, there could be no lasting damage from the tortures he would have to endure. All that he must do to win the ruby firestone was to take whatever pain Chom inflicted on him from sunrise to sunset.

He didn't stop to consider where and how Chom had gotten the ruby in the first place. That was not his concern.

Nor did he consider what he might possess that Chom wanted badly enough to risk the gem. He had won many treasures in the body-betting, any one of which might tempt a Shegrin.

There was also the glory of winning the wager.

Gonar was Champion of Jhent, the winner of more body-bets than anyone in fifty years. To break him would be a great accomplishment. Anyone who could do it would have every Shegrin in the Kingdom at his door offering wagers. The prospect was not only tempting, it was downright delicious.

Gonar held up a bronze hand mirror and practiced his smile once again. It was a disarming smile, a confident smile. His white teeth flashed in his black, curly beard and his gray eyes sparkled like sunlight on rainwater beneath his broad, even brow. He lifted his aquiline nose with just a hint of arrogance.

Confidence was important in Shegri. The right smile, just as one's opponent inflicted some excruciating pain, could break the opponent, force him into concession. It was as much a game of nerve as it was of endurance.

Gonar put the mirror down and picked up his heavy, wool cloak. Some people wore more than the cloak to the match, but Gonar's body was good enough that he didn't feel the need to ornament it. Let Chom admire his muscles, his heavy balls, his big, thick cock, right from the start! Basking in admiration was also a weapon in the play.

He put on his cloak and drew its scarlet length around him, covering his body completely, then left his house.

■ ■ ■ ■

The arena was at the center of Jhent's capital city of Jhentfel, to one side of the royal palace. It had been established there for as long as anyone could remember, for the kings of Jhent had always been patrons of Shegri and had frequently made great wagers on the outcome of a hotly contested match.

Gonar was proud to have earned the King a number of prizes in the days before His Majesty had come under the influence of the peculiar new god, Dworkrimian, whose dark temple was built at the north end of the city. Now Gonar entered the arena from the side opposite the palace, for there were always black-robed Dworkist priests and priestesses proselytizing near the King's abode, and they were vociferous in their disapproval of Shegri.

He descended to the maze of corridors beneath the main floor of the arena and made his way toward the scrying chamber at the very center, returning the cheerful greetings of his many admirers who worked there as he went. Outside the chamber he dropped three coins into the basin that rested at the feet of the statue of Roghgota, the deity traditionally worshipped in Jhent. He said a brief prayer of thanksgiving for his past victories, and another, slightly longer one, asking victory in the match forthcoming. Then he went in.

Chom was already there, as were the Soothsayer and the Prophetess who waited to scry his health. He greeted them all, shrugged off his cloak, and stepped into the charmed circle at the center of the chamber. The old man and the older woman began their magical examination of him, walking slowly around and around.

Chom eyed his body with obvious admiration and Gonar felt a warm glow.

Chom was a little taller than Gonar. His hair was also dark, shot with auburn hints, and his eyes were black, like polished lumps of coal. His beard was cut close to his chin, his nose was short, and his complexion was olive. His musculature was not so rounded as Gonar's but he was clearly strong, a corded man with long limbs. He wore the crossed leather harness and velvet loincloth of a Tilesian Corsair, and if that did not mark him for a seafarer the hoop of gold from which a polished ruby depended most surely did.

Gonar noted that the velvet loincloth seemed to be well filled. He also noted that Chom's short fur cloak was fastened at the shoulder with a brooch containing the ruby firestone.

The Soothsayer and the Prophetess continued to walk around and around Gonar, gazing intently at his flesh. The slightest oddity of color, a wrongness in his muscle tone and they would be able to tell. They would use their powers to look into him, to descry any trace of the herbs a dishonorable Shegrin might take to ward off pain. If they found such a trace it would be grounds for disqualification.

Gonar had no worry on that account. For him, honor was a part of glory. Prizes were worthless to him if they were not fairly won. He loved his sport, and he loved the challenge of pitting his own strength against his own weakness. It was not, not really, Chom who was his adversary. No, it was himself whom he must conquer, and no better match could be made in any sport than pitting a man against himself.

After a while the two inspectors nodded approval and each touched a palm to the place over his heart to give him their seal. Gonar stepped out of the circle and smiled at Chom.

"May you have good fortune before the gods," he said, the formula friendly and meant honestly.

"And you," said Chom, his voice smooth and dark. They clenched their fists and touched them together with a little knock, right to left, right to left, then a slave handed Gonar his cloak and he wrapped it about himself. A door opened opposite the one he had entered and the dim light of pre-dawn filtered down the broad stairway that led up into the arena.

Gonar went up first.

■ ■ ■ ■

The arena was filled with people and as Gonar emerged a cheer went up. He was favored as both champion and native son, and the bets rode heavily on him. He raised his arms in greeting and the cheer grew to thunder. He danced around in a circle as he walked to the equipment, smiling up to the people all around him. He reached the equipment and his practiced eye took in everything at a glance: pulleys and straps and wheels and low tables with whips. It was all very standard stuff. His confidence increased.

Chom came up into the arena and the sound of the crowd was less welcoming. Gonar looked at his opponent and thought that it would have been better if he had some support in the stands. He was a handsome man, deserving of better than jeers.

The judges came from either side in their blue silk robes and raised their wands for silence. The crowd quieted. The judges, and Gonar and Chom, bowed to the King and his Queen in their high box. Gonar noted that one of the Dworkist priests stood at the King's shoulder, his mouth twisted in a sour smirk of contempt. The priest was slight of build, a man who could not have stood up to even an hour of Shegri.

"You know the rules," the eldest judge said, in a voice that carried to all. "You, Gonar, must submit to whatever Chom chooses to do to you: from the moment of sunrise to the moment of sunset. You must not call halt or you will lose the bet. You, Chom, may do whatever you wish to Gonar's body; but you must not do anything that will cause a scar or cause any other permanent damage.

"And you!" he said to the crowd. "You all must keep absolute silence! If anyone speaks or in any other ways disturbs the contest, that person will be ejected from the arena and never, never be allowed to return! Bets must be made either in silence or outside the arena.

"By your presence here you do consent to these rules! Be advised, and keep the peace! Let the contest begin!"

The judges stepped back to either side. Gonar unfastened the clasp of his cloak and handed the cloak to Chom, symbolically giving himself into his challenger's hands. Chom took it courteously and laid it over the stand that had been provided for that purpose.

For a moment Chom stood looking at Gonar's naked body, softly lit by the morning light. It was a moment Gonar always relished: the moment when the whole populace looked down upon his nakedness with admiration and with mounting lust. He liked to be desired. He felt his heavy cock stir, as it always did. Then the rim of the sun blazed above the eastern wall of the arena and the contest began.

Chom took a length of rawhide and wrapped it around Gonar's wrists. It was the weaker of the two beginnings, but that told Gonar little. Had Chom tied his hands behind him the possibilities of suspension would have been more limited.

Chom made twenty circuits of the wrists, then wrapped the thong the other way, between hands and wrists, to provide separation. He tied off the leather with a neat knot and asked if Gonar's circulation was impaired.

"No," Gonar responded.

"Good. Now come here," Chom said.

He led Gonar to a large framework of pulleys and wooden beams. He attached Gonar's wrists to a hook suspended from a rope which led upward to a pulley. Then Chom pulled a wooden pin from one of the beams, releasing a huge stone attached to the rope. Gonar's arms were pulled upward and he was lifted slightly from the ground.

Chom now took a few moments to fit other boards into the frame. These were thin, almost knife-edged boards that he arranged in slots to form an open-sided cylinder behind Gonar. Through adjustments in the positions of the boards, Gonar saw, it was possible to make the cylinder's diameter smaller and smaller, the boards' sharp edges closer together.

Chom smiled at Gonar and released another stone. This time the counterbalances of the apparatus pulled Gonar backward, so that the sharp blades of the cylinder pressed against his back and broad shoulders painfully.

Next Chom attached leather manacles to Gonar's ankles, manacles fitted with metal rings and lined with sheepskin. He fastened ropes to the metal rings and released two or more stones, and Gonar's feet were drawn backward and up, so that his butt and the backs of his legs were pressed tight against the sharp boards of the cylinder. He was now bent backward in a circle around the device, his arms together but his legs spread wide apart.

He felt his cock grow very stiff. He knew that in the stands people would be beginning to squirm, their mouths watering. His balls hung heavily downward, so exposed that he knew they would be Chom's next object of attack.

Chom took a length of rawhide and wrapped it around Gonar's balls, again and again, forming a tube as he stretched them downward. With the last of the rawhide he made a crosstie that separated Gonar's balls, forcing them apart. Then he tied the end with another neat knot. He took a small leather noose from the table and slipped it over the stretched balls, tightened it, and, smiling, tied the other end to a large stone which he hefted in his hand. His black eyes flashed at Gonar and he dropped the stone.

Pain stabbed at Gonar like a spear thrust up through his groin. He twitched, but he kept the smile on his face, matching Chom's pleasantry. He was used to this kind of pain. Shegrin usually tried ball torture early in the game, as it was easy. Knowing this, Gonar had inflicted much greater agonies on himself by way of practice.

Chom nodded, as if he expected no more. He reached out, took Gonar's big cock in his hand, squeezed it, stroked it up and down a couple of times, then bent and planted a kiss on the head of it. Then he turned away to find another tool.

For just a second Gonar felt himself unsure. The touch of Chom's hand, the stroking, the kiss, were not a part of the usual approach. Shegrin never did things that were comforting or affectionate—and the feel of Chom's hand: it had not been painful, but somehow hot, as if glazed with fire. How had Chom done that?

Chom pulled another pin and Gonar felt himself stretched tighter, his arms now downward, his feet drawn up toward them. The wooden blades bit into his body and the sun, now well clear of the arena wall, burnt into his eyes.

"You might wish to think," said Chom quietly, "about which of your many treasures it is that I want. I can assure you that it will be the most valuable of them by far."

Gonar smiled, turning his head to his adversary, against the stretch of his neck muscles.

"I can assure you that you will not get it," he said cheerfully, "and that your ruby will make a fine addition to my collection."

They both chuckled. The interchange put things back in place for Gonar, as it was the kind of talk the betters usually made during the contest. And yet—there was something odd about the way Chom spoke. As if...

Gonar shook off the doubt that was creeping in. Perhaps an oddity of manner was the "trick" that Chom hoped to use to win. If so, Gonar thought, he would be disappointed!

Chom addressed himself to Gonar's nipples. He brushed his fingers lightly back and forth across them, stimulating them, and Gonar felt them stiffen. It was a delicious sensation, more so than it had any right to be. There was just that hint of fire ... But what was so special about Chom's fingers?

Chom presented two small, wooden clips for Gonar's inspection. They had little screws that would allow them to be tightened. He put them on Gonar's nipples and turned the screws just enough that they would not pull off when he tugged at them.

Chom went around in back and after a moment Gonar felt a probing at his asshole. He loosened his sphincter, knowing well the mistake of resisting anything that might be done to him. He felt something small and hard and cylindrical slip in smoothly, slippery, as if Chom had greased it to make the entry easier. This was decidedly out of character for a Shegrin. Just what did Chom have in mind?

Gonar closed his eyes and calmed himself. It was silly, even dangerous, to question. What would come, would come. The future was forbidden territory. There was only the now and the past.

Chom came back around front and looked Gonar over. He seemed satisfied. He went to the table on which the smaller implements were arranged and opened a little wooden box. From the box he removed a blown glass vial. He held it up so that the sunlight illuminated its ruby swirls. He came and held it before Gonar, then pulled the stopper and a long, glass rod from which dripped a glistening, viscous liquid.

Chom set the vial on the ground and took Gonar's hard cock in his hand. He leaned over and kissed the head again, ran his tongue over it, then straightened and began to work the glass rod into Gonar's piss hole.

The pain was instantaneous. It felt as if Chom were shoving a red-hot poker into Gonar's cock. Gonar's every muscle went tense as he strained against his bonds. He clenched his teeth.

Chom smiled at the reaction and continued to slide the rod in, wiggling it back and forth, pulling it a little out, pushing deeper in.

Gonar felt the sweat break out on his face, in his armpits. The agony grew, his gut invaded with burning coals.

Gonar opened his eyes wide and looked straight into the sun, letting the lances of light that drove into his retinas tear his mind and nerves away from the pain in his prick. He let the sun torture him, force his attention away from Chom's torturing.

After a moment the pain in his dick ceased to get worse. It did not abate, but it didn't get any worse, and he could tolerate it. He let the air out of his lungs and began to breathe deeply. He knew that if he could get air moving through his blood steadily it would lessen the pain.

Chom slipped a thread through a tiny hole in the end of the glass rod that stuck out of Gonar's prick, then looped it around the head of Gonar's prick and secured it, so that the rod would not slide out.

Gonar bared his teeth in his best grin, smiling up at the sun but meaning it for Chom.

Chom picked up the vial, put his thumb over the opening, upended it, then yanked the clips off Gonar's tits. With the pain fresh, he rubbed the burning liquid on both of Gonar's tits, then replaced the clamps, tightening them just a little more as the fire ate away.

Chom went around back and Gonar knew what was coming next. He concentrated on his breathing, forcing his breath to slow, using the exercise he had learned from a midwife. He forced air into his bloodstream with careful breathing, the way a woman was told to in childbirth. He felt the small plug slide out of his asshole.

Chom came to the front and held up the plug, letting Gonar watch as he smeared the liquid all over the plug with his thumb. It was the basic anticipation ploy, and Gonar was not particularly impressed. He continued to modulate his breath.

Then Chom slid the anointed plug up his ass and the fire struck and it was all that Gonar could do to keep from crying out. His body thrashed as a feeling like shovels of hot coals burned into his bowels.

He stared into the sun. Then he wrenched his mind from the point of pain in his asshole to the one in his cock, to the two fires burning his tits. He called silently on the gods, but that made it worse: he remembered the tale of the hero who had been fucked by the volcano god, and he knew what it was like to have jet after jet of molten lava squirting deep into him. Sweat broke out all over him.

When he noticed the sweat he found a way out. He forced his mind away from his body completely and tried to imagine what he must look like to the crowd, glistening with sweat, bound to Chom's torture rack, twisting in agony under the full light of the sun. He thought about how he would respond to the sight of himself thus stretched and tortured, and he found that the pain in his cock was suddenly superseded by the pleasure as it stiffened more.

He was safe.

He had conquered the moment. The pain was bearable.

A lash landed across his back, between the sharp blades of the rack, brought up hard within the open cylinder. He nearly screamed with surprise, but then its many-thonged tongue licked at him again and he nearly laughed. He knew the kiss of the lash like the touch of an old lover!

Between the blades of the rack the whipping continued, each stroke landing on a different part of his body. His back knew it, then his butt, his shoulders, his thighs, his calves. Then again. He knew better than to count, but it did not seem long before Chom ceased to whip him.

Had the Corsair's arm worn out so quickly, or did Chom see that it was having no effect?

Chom's rough, strong hand moved over his back, his shoulders, his butt, his legs, gently, rubbing on something oily. The fire struck, ripping into his new welts like salt into sword wounds. Each stroke was an inferno. He thrashed, twisted, strained. He fought against the groan in his throat.

So this was Chom's secret! A bottle that turned everything into fiery pain!

Let him burn me! Gonar railed in his mind.

Let him burn me, let him whip me! I will prevail against him as I have prevailed against all the others. Neither fire nor ice will open my lips!

And then Gonar used another of the tricks he had developed for winning the game, one that could not be copied through observation, for it was strictly a trick of the mind.

He struggled into the past, away from the now, searching for a moment of triumph to cancel out what felt like present defeat. In his head was a vast warehouse stacked with victories, and he knew that it offered both escape and the power of defense.

Neither fire nor ice, he had cried out to himself.

And in the memory of ice he saw his strategy.

He drew out the memory of Tarkors of Thremfel, the northern barbarian who had challenged him in winter.

Though Jhent never froze, Tarkors had brought down ice from the mountains: ice and snow packed in sawdust to keep it from melting. Tarkors had packed him in ice from the neck down and waited for him to beg mercy.

But Tarkors had been an honorable man, and when he had seen that Gonar's life was threatened he had pulled him out of the ice and clasped him against his own warm body to revive him.

From Tarkors Gonar had won much glory and a fine suit of brazen scale armor as well. He had coughed and sneezed for weeks, but he had won the bet! And now...

Gonar drew out the memory of what it felt like to freeze. He let the flesh of him slow, let the cold bite into him bitterly from the past, let the blueness creep into his bones.

Chom came to the front and lifted the rock that hung from Gonar's balls. He took the noose off, untied the thong, and released Gonar's balls from their bondage. He massaged the big balls, then knelt and licked them.

Gonar felt himself drawn out of his reverie. Again, Chom was doing something that was not a part of the game, not until now. Something affectionate in the middle of his assault. But by now Gonar recognized it as a technique, a way of preparing him for some more intense pain. He sought to retreat into the warehouse of memory again.

Chom stopped licking, then rubbed the fire liquid on Gonar's balls. The fire took hold, singeing, searing. Chom wrapped the thong back around the balls, stretched them, put the noose back on, selected a stone twice as large as the previous one, and, looking into Gonar's face, dropped it.

A flaming sword stabbed up into Gonar's groin. A grunt escaped his lips. Chom's eyes were black fires, terrible and beautiful.

Chom put more liquid on his thumb, then shoved it into Gonar's mouth, smearing it around liberally. The fire took hold of his tongue. Then Chom stuck his little finger into the vial and smeared the liquid into both of Gonar's nostrils.

None of the pain that had come before had prepared Gonar for the conflagration that ignited in his nasal passages. Not only did the liquid burn where it touched, the very smell of it burned, up into his head with each breath he took.

He screamed.

"Will you yield?" Chom asked, intensely, close to his ear.

For a moment Gonar felt that he must resign the contest, that if he did not the whole top of his head would be torn off. But when he turned to Chom to speak the fateful word, he saw the look on Chom's face and he bit it back. Chom's eyes were eager, triumphant. Chom was hungry for his own glory and for Gonar's defeat.

"No!" Gonar screamed, letting the word take the pain out of him.

He wrenched his gaze away from Chom's face, running from his opponent's victory, and fastened on the Royal Box, instinctively seeking his defense in his fealty.

But what was there?

He saw the face of the High Priest of Dworkrimian, and something clutched at his heart. The priest still maintained the sourness of his mouth, but there was something else, something in his eyes. It was as if...

Chom pulled three of the wooden slats and suddenly the cylinder over which Gonar was bent back was decreased. He was stretched tighter, his back bent more painfully.

Chom slipped a black leather hood over his eyes and the brightness of the sunlight on his face disappeared. There were no eyeholes in the hood, barely enough ventilation for him to breathe. There was almost no sound, as his ears were padded.

So, Gonar thought desperately, Chom knew how a man might escape into the sights and sounds around him, and was now cutting off that line of retreat. Well, let him! He could not close the doors of the mind.

Chom's hands moved over his body, smearing on something that soon covered his chest, his arms, his legs.

Gonar found himself hoping that it was the fire liquid. If it were, if the pain were made general, then the intensity in the various parts would decrease. Chom would be doing him a favor!

He braced himself against the coming pain, concentrating on the sweet smell of the leather that came through the burning smell in his nose, feeling intensely the supple leather pressing against his face. There was pleasure in the coolness of darkness that eased the light pain in his eyes.

But where was the burning on his chest? The fire was not taking hold, and Chom's hands had left his body.

Something moved by his ear and sound returned.

"I have put something different on you, Gonar, on that part of your body that faces the sun. It will not burn you of itself, but the rays of the sun now will. It is a lotion like the ruby firestone you so covet. It amplifies the light and slowly cooks your flesh. I think that sometime you must have been sunburned. Do you remember how it poisons you? Do you remember the week that follows, when you cannot sit or sleep but in pain? Even a lover's touch will be an agony for that time. There will be no possibility of comfort. Think how it will be to have your cock raw with sunburn, Gonar, my Gonar."

Gonar felt Chom's hand on his cock, squeezing, then gently stroking it. Chom stroked well, he noted, almost counteracting the pain of the rod inside. Then he felt Chom's tongue, his mouth. Chom took his whole cock into his mouth.

Roghgota! Gonar swore silently. The man was more adept at sex than he was at torture!

The mouth moved away and he heard Chom once again at his ear.

"Gonar, my Gonar, I shall tear out your soul today and take it home with me in a box!"

The padding went back in by his ear and for a moment Gonar felt all his sensations, both pleasure and pain, slip away. What did Chom mean? What was Chom saying, so strange and different from anything any Shegrin had ever said before?

A whip landed across Gonar's belly, hard. His muscles tensed, fought against his bonds. The whip landed again. Again he felt safe, back in the realm of normal pain, of the kind of contest he was used to. He had known the whip all his life, from the affectionate beatings that his parents had given him to the punishments meted out in his war training. He almost laughed to think of any soldier being bothered by a mere whipping.

The leather of the whip bit into his upper chest, his lower belly, then his arms, the fronts of his thighs, his shins. Chom knew how to use a whip, how to inflict pain without damage. The man was highly skilled. Gonar had to admire him, even as he delivered each terrible stroke ... What a lover Chom would make!

The whipping stopped. Gonar, not a tiny spot of his body now without pain, forced himself to relax. He had to let the blood flow into his tissue before the next onslaught.

Once more the padding was removed from one ear and Chom's voice spoke darkly and quietly: "The sun has moved, Gonar. I will have to move you, to keep your beautiful body facing it. To let the sun have its full effect on you."

Gonar felt the engine on which he was racked move; felt the sun fall hotter across his chest, his belly, his cock. Then, after a pause, he felt Chom tighten the clamps on his nipples.

It was time, Gonar felt, to go away. To search in earnest through the warehouse of his memories.

He ranged back, looking for times and feelings that were as intense as the present. He found C'Teil, the black man from the far south who had set insects all over his body. He found the twins, Vrabeg and Cunbeg, who had hung him upside down over a cauldron of boiling herbs that made him dizzy and sick until he puked.

Chom slid the plug out of his asshole and pushed in another, much larger one, stretching the hole painfully and inflicting more fire; but Gonar embraced the memory of Colodon, who had impaled him on a rough stake and whipped him for hours with flat leather whips that left no mark. Chom slid the plug in and out, fucking him with fire, but Gonar withstood it, searching wildly through the corridors of thought.

The sun got hotter and hotter. He felt the sweat pouring off his body, the burn eating it. It would be a painful week ahead, but the ruby firestone would compensate for it. More than that, the look of defeat in Chom's black eyes would be ultimate triumph; for Gonar realized now that Chom was the best opponent he had ever had!

The fucking stopped.

Gonar felt the rack move again, the sun intensify.

Then a deeper darkness fell over his head, a richer coolness. There was a time of silence. Then:

A terrible throbbing pain born out of sound!

Chom had put a bell over his head, and now he struck it, sending waves of violent pain through the very bones of Gonar's skull, so loud, so awful, that had it not been for the padding over his ears he would have been struck deaf on the instant. Gonar screamed, but his scream was eaten up in the ringing of the bell. All the doorways in his mind slammed shut and he was thrust into the present, clamped under the inescapable agony of the ringing.

Later he knew that if he could have made himself heard he would have surrendered in that one moment. But the noise was so complete, the pain so total, that there was not even the hope of capitulation. He screamed and screamed again.

Abruptly the big butt plug was yanked out of his ass, another, larger one was shoved in, the hammer struck the bell and jellied his brain, and something jerked on his balls, all at once. A final strike upon the bell and starry darkness, unconsciousness, swept over him.

■ ■ ■ ■

When he awoke the pain was still there in all of its particulars; except for the banging of the bell. His sphincter was stretched by an unimaginably large plug that delved deep into his bowels. The fiery liquid was all through him. The weight on his balls was heavier and he could feel big stones lying on his chest, stretching his nipples painfully. The rod was still in his cock and the welts all over his body now ached as well as burning. He could feel the sunburn on his cock, and on his chest and belly ... But something was wrong. Despite the fiery pain he was cool.

He sorted his pains and forced his mind to reason.

There was no sunlight falling on him at all. The air was still warm, but the sunlight was gone. That meant the sun had gone down behind the far side of the arena.

How long had he been unconscious?

He tried to figure out how long the torture had gone on before he had passed out, but torture always played havoc with subjective time. Moments could seem like eternities when one was in pain.

He had never before been rendered unconscious.

But then, he had never before had an opponent like Chom. Gonar tried to speak, feeling his tongue blistered and hampered by the confines of the leather hood.

"Chom?"

There was no answer.

"Chom?"

He calmed himself, drew in breath through his still-burning nostrils. Something was seriously wrong. Chom should have answered him, if only with the renewed infliction of pain.

"Chom!" he cried out.

He felt a hand wrap around his cock, warm and firm. Chom spoke into his ear, his dark voice soft, sinister.

"Gonar, my Gonar, you are mine. To do with as I will. Now the torture can really begin!"

The hand moved away and Gonar felt a moment of panic. What did Chom mean? What was going on?

A cool breeze blew lightly across his chest.

Gonar felt a chill run through his whole frame. For the breeze to have actually cooled at this time of year it must be well past sunset, well into the night. If that were the case, then the contest was over and he had won. He should have been released!

Or had he won?

He sent his mind racing backward. The last thing he remembered was the terrible bell clanging over his head. There had been darkness. He remembered screaming, remembered being willing to give in, if only he could be heard over the sound.

Had he then called halt? Had he actually called out the word; and had it been heard?

He could not remember doing it. He did not think that he had.

But even if he had resigned the contest, why was he still bound, still under torture? It was long after sunset. The contest was over!

Chom's words sprang into his mind as if written on basalt with red lightning: Now you are mine. To do with as I will.

Chom had promised to take the most valuable thing he possessed. Would the rules of the contest allow the victor to take the man himself? To make the loser his slave?

The breeze grew colder and Gonar felt a chill that was not of the night, making his blood run like ice. If Chom had him as slave, and he was still bound, and Chom had promised that the torture would now begin...

The sweat that seeped from his pores this time was clammy, cold. His heart beat fiercely. Such a prize was not part of the sport as he knew it! It went beyond all traditions! How could the King allow...

He remembered the light in the eyes of the High Priest of Dworkrimian. The Dworkists were reputed to have cruelties of their own, cruelties jealously guarded by their god. Was the light in the priest's eyes akin to the dark light in Chom's eyes? Who was this Chom, and whence came he? Could it be that he was in league with the Dworkist priesthood? If so, such a variance from tradition might well have the King's ear!

He thought of the volcano god, hungry for human sacrifice. How much did he know of Dworkrimian? What rites were so attractive that the King had abandoned the god of his ancestors?

A moan escaped his lips.

He felt Chom's hand on his cock, affectionate, terrible. He felt the string untied from around the head, felt the rod slide slowly out. He felt Chom's mouth on his dick, felt Chom's tongue flick at his piss hole.

"Let me hear you say it again, my beautiful victim," Chom crooned from the region of his groin. Chom's voice was weird, like that of a madman.

Gonar bit his tongue, the fear like frost crystallizing over his body. He felt Chom's mouth slide over his cock, suck it, swallow it. The feeling was exquisite, yet it roused only his terror. What was Chom preparing him for this time?

Chom's mouth left his cock. He felt the weight released from his balls, the noose removed, the thong untied. He felt his balls hang loose. He felt Chom lick them.

"Come, let me hear you say it! " Chom urged. "The sound of your voice is sweet to me, crying out halt. I love that sound, that word that gives me victory, that delivers you into my power completely!"

Gonar sobbed, held back the word that was struggling to get out. It was useless now, and there was no point in it. If he had said it once, he would not say it again.

Chom yanked the weighted clips roughly off his tits. "Speak!" Chom commanded, and then his tongue flicked fiercely over Gonar's nipples.

Gonar's whole body ached, raged with the pains inflicted on it, and the memory of them was fresh. Each touch from Chom brought him to the recent past, to the past of the torture, and threw him back against the present, and the possible future. What more could Chom do to him? What more would Chom do?

If the contest was over, then he was no longer protected by the rules!

Chom's fingers moved over his body, lightly touching the welts and the sunburn. It was delicate, soft— an agony!

"If you beg me, I may choose to stop," Chom said. "I have told you that I will rip your soul from your body. Why not give it to me willingly? I may be merciful."

Gonar was terrified as he had never been in battle. Nothing like this had ever happened to him. He had never imagined it. Chom seemed to have desires that were beyond his understanding. He thought again of the High Priest of Dworkrimian, and remembered that the Corsairs of Tilesia were reputed to worship many, many gods.

Chom's fingers moved to his back and Chom's body moved against him. Gonar felt his opponent's strong muscles against his chest, the crossed leather harness of the Corsair. Encased in the velvet loincloth he felt Chom's large, hard cock press against his balls. Chom's fingers moved over the burning welts on his back, like spiders. "Speak!" Chom urged, grinding his hard cock against Gonar's balls, his fingers creeping down Gonar's back. "Speak!"

Gonar felt the urgency of Chom's desire and his mind shattered. To be owned by a madman crazed with unintelligible lusts, on the verge of tortures more dreadful than all the things he had ever endured: it was unbearable.

Chom's fingers reached his buttocks. They took hold of the huge plug and began to fuck his ass with it, slowly, deeply, each stroke almost all the way out, each stroke all the way in, a cock of white, hot bronze.

"Soon I will begin to hurt you, " Chom said, and he licked Gonar's throat and slid the plug all the way out of his asshole. "Please...," Gonar mumbled.

Chom moved away from him, left him stretched and suspended in cool darkness. All the implements were gone from his body. Only the wooden blades bit into his bent back. He was naked, ready for whatever was next.

"Let me hear it!" Chom commanded, triumph in his voice. "Let me hear it!"

Gonar felt something touch his left nipple, ever so slightly.

"Halt!" he said, crumbling. Then he cried out into the darkness of the black leather hood. "Halt!"

It was like the falling of a citadel. The gates of his pride went down. The salve of submission flowed over him and he felt everything in him flow out. To his surprise, his cock stiffened painfully and the built-up flood of his semen burst forth. His balls shrank up into him and he shot, painful bolts of cum spurting out of him as everything he had ever been caved in on him. Up the hard tunnel of his prick, through its burning stretched walls, out its violated slit.

He knew himself for slave.

And then it got worse.

There was applause.

Cheers, whistles, cries of approval. He felt the lacing on the hood being undone, then the hood was torn from his head. Blinding light fell against his eyes—but not direct light. Above him, cutting off the sun's rays, was a large screen of black leather, a canopy. He was bound in its shadow. To either side of him, and in back and front, were stacked blocks of ice. A weighted fan blew air across the ice to produce the cool breezes of late night.

It was not much past noon.

His spirit rose. He felt suddenly elated, as if he had been delivered from the hands of the death god. He had lost the wager, had been defeated, had submitted himself to Chom completely; but it had been fair. Chom had tortured his mind, even as he had used his mind for defense. Chom had won! Gonar felt his limbs contract painfully as Chom reversed the balancing of stones and released him from his stretched posture. In a moment his ankles and hands were free and he staggered, standing once more on the beaten earth of the arena. Then Chom stood before him, smiling, and the disquiet invaded him again. There was still that look in Chom's eyes, that look so like...

"Come forth!" a herald cried from the Royal Box. Gonar stepped forward but his legs were yet too weak to support him. He stumbled and Chom caught him. Chom's touch on his body was like new fire, and Gonar's mind fell apart again. He stumbled toward the King and Queen, now totally under the Corsair's spell.

"You have won, Chom of Tilesia," King Rhanges said with dignity. "State for us the terms of the wager."

Gonar pulled himself upright, standing on his own feet. Chom let him go and stepped a little forward.

"I have wagered the ruby firestone in my brooch," Chom said. "I have won, and so I will have as my price a pair of matched jewels which Gonar possesses."

Gonar tried, still groggy, to think of where in his collection of treasure there might be a pair of matched jewels ... Then the truth hit him.

"Do you mean...," asked the King.

"Yes," Chom said calmly, reaching and seizing Gonar's balls in his hand. "These."

There was a roar from the stands. People did not wager in this way in Jhent: and yet, there was a fascination in the idea. The roar of the crowd turned from one of shock and horror, ever so slowly, to one of admiration. Finally cheers rose up. They wanted blood.

Gonar felt the cold creeping into his stomach, the color draining from his face. These were his own people!

King Rhanges looked confused.

The priest of Dworkrimian leaned forward, his eyes blazing with triumph, and whispered to the King.

Gonar fought the darkness in his belly. It was bad enough to lose, then to have the crowd cheer for his emasculation. He would not faint before them! The King raised his arms for silence and the roar stilled.

"People of Jhent!" the King said, his voice harsh. "Here Us! Gonar has been Champion of Jhent, and your hero, in many contests in this arena. Now a new man comes here and asks for Gonar's very manhood as his prize. Yet do you cry out your anger? No! You cry for the blood of your favorite son! We, your King, are ashamed of you! What has this sport made of you that you think a man's body worth as little as a pretty trinket? This priest of Dworkrimian has long counseled that the pain of a man's body is not fit subject for sport, and now We agree with him! Gonar's manhood shall not be a prize in a bloody game! Nor shall this impious game continue! If some of you wish to offer your flesh to the torture, take it to the temple of Dworkrimian, or offer it to Roghgota, but this arena shall no longer harbor torture as a sport! We have spoken!"

Without even looking down on the contestants again, the King turned and left his box, followed by the Queen, the Royal guards and the smiling priest of Dworkrimian.

...And a good thing, too, Gonar thought. For as the shock of the King's proclamation swept through the crowd, the

arena went wild. The people of Jhent had been robbed of
their favorite pastime. They turned mean. The judges in their
blue robes waved their wands and tried to restore order, but
it was useless.

Gonar stood stock-still, sick with conflicting passions,
wondering if they blamed him for what had happened. He
had not tried to back out of the wager, but he was sure that
at any moment there would be a riot, and that his emasculation would come at the hands of the mob.

The mob, which did nothing but watch!

Death he did not fear. Death was an old friend to any
soldier. But shame made him sick, and contempt made him
angry. The matter was between him and Chom, not between
the King and the people, and the gods.

He turned and looked at Chom.

And Chom, the precipitator of all this, the weird hero of
the day, acted in a way that was more terrible than anything
anyone could have imagined. He raised his arms for silence,
just as the King had.

And, because he was a weird hero in the middle of chaos,
he got silence.

"People of Jhent!" Chom said, and his voice was as rich
and reaching as that of any herald or king. "Your ruler has
made a new law. The Corsairs of Tilesia have long made
their way in the world by upholding, for pay, the laws of
many kingdoms. I say to you that you must follow the King's
word, even if I am cheated by its utterance!"

The crowd made a sound like the growling in the throat
of a tiger, but Chom continued.

"If you feel the honor of your Kingdom is thus tainted,
it is between you and your King, not upon the head of your
champion, Gonar, who acted in all good faith in making his
wager. It may also be between you and your gods, for it
was the King's advisor who sought this new law ... That is
none of my concern, for I honor all gods, wherever I
travel."

The growling of the crowd quieted, changed tone.

"In the morning I shall leave Jhent, and I shall have no regrets. I came here honestly, I have enjoyed the sport provided me, and I shall go with as much as I brought. I could have left without my firestone had I lost."

He smiled.

"I shall tell the world of the honorable Gonar, and how well he stood my testing. I shall also tell of the changes which your King has decreed. If ever I return, I shall be interested to see what further changes have been made!"

He turned and walked toward the exit and the crowd became silent, paying him the only tribute it could offer for a moment.

Then, as he reached the stairs, the applause started. He did not turn back as it rolled to thunder. He disappeared into the darkness below.

■■■■

The streets were dark and finally silent, the rioting against the King's new law put down, when Gonar entered the house that Chom occupied. Gonar had eaten and washed and anointed himself with the best scented oils, as he would have done when going to the Temple of Roghgota. Otherwise he was cloaked as he would have been for the arena, naked beneath. Chom was waiting for him, seated before a small brazier drinking spiced wine.

"I knew you would come," Chom said.

"Yes," Gonar answered. "I was certain that you knew that."

"Your honor was what attracted me to you in the first place, many years ago. I was here and watching from the stands when Tarkors packed you in ice. It was he who gave me the idea for the piles of ice, to make you think it was late night. I fanned them as hard as I could to make the cool breezes."

Gonar smiled.

"I thought of Tarkors while you were torturing me. If I had but known..."

"But I misled you," said Chom. "I chose my words carefully, and I misled you."

"Yes," said Gonar, "but it was fair."

He took off the long, red cloak and handed it to Chom, once again surrendering himself to his opponent. Chom took it courteously and laid it across a chair. He gestured, and for the first time Gonar noticed the equipment prepared for him. A chair with manacles on the arms. Across from it a set of stocks that would hold his legs very far apart. On the little brazier a very sharp knife whose blade glowed dull red.

Gonar went and sat in the chair. Chom fastened his arms down tight. Gonar stretched out his legs and Chom fastened his ankles into the stocks. His balls hung over the edge of the chair.

Chom took a smaller stock, very small, with a single hole through the center. He stretched Gonar's balls way down and fastened the little stock around them. Now they were separated from Gonar's groin by a heavy thickness of wood. Gonar felt a slight beading of sweat form on his forehead, in his armpits.

"Gonar, my Gonar," Chom whispered. "I told you that I would rip your soul out of you, didn't I?"

Gonar nodded, and swallowed hard.

Chom fell to his knees and fastened his mouth on Gonar's cock. He sucked, he tongued, he swallowed, and Gonar felt at last the unleashed fury of Chom's passion. He had been right: Chom was a better lover than he was a torturer. Gonar felt the explosion building in him ... But he expected it when Chom backed off, stood, and went to get the red-hot knife.

"Do you freely yield to me my due?" Chom asked as he knelt again, placing the blade very near to Gonar's balls.

Gonar nodded.

"Say it!"

"I freely yield to you my ... balls," Gonar said. "You have won them fairly."

"They are mine?" Chom asked.

"They are yours," Gonar answered.

"To do with as I wish, always?" Chom continued, and Gonar felt the heat of the knife, close.

"Always, to do with as you wish," said Gonar. He clenched his teeth. He would not shut his eyes but he could not look down.

The hot knife touched, searing.

Then Chom pulled it away and stood. "I will take them, now," Chom said, and that strange, burning light came into his eyes. "But I would rather have them with the rest of you attached."

There was silence in the room, and Gonar understood what the whole thing was about. Why Chom had said the things he had in the arena. Why he had done what he had done. Gonar knew what the strange force was that made Chom's hands like fire.

It was not a thing spoken between men who were not warriors, and when it was spoken it was only in private.

"You love me?" Gonar asked.

"I will own you as a man, or no one shall!" Chom said, passionately, but shy of the actual speaking.

Gonar felt himself sink, felt himself joyously submit to the will of the only man who had ever broken him. But he had a small shred of pride left, and now he satisfied it.

"Say it!" Gonar demanded.

"I love you," said Chom.

Gonar let out one long, shuddering breath.

"I yield my body to you," he said. "Freely do I yield it, to do with as you wish, always."

"And?" Chom queried.

For a moment Gonar was confused. Then it became clear.

"And my soul," he said.

Chom knelt before him again, brought the blade close.

"Oh, Gonar, my Gonar," he whispered hoarsely. But it was his tongue that touched Gonar's balls, not the knife. Then his tongue was upon Gonar's cock, his mouth engulfing it. Then upon his belly, his chest, his lips. The velvet of Chom's loincloth pressed against Gonar's face and he felt Chom's great, hard prick. The velvet was yanked away and Chom's beautiful cock pushed between Gonar's lips, plunged into his throat.

Gonar sucked, struggled to master the passions of the man who now owned him. But as he tasted Chom's weapon stiffening, preparing to shoot, it was pulled out of his mouth and he stared into Chom's blazing black eyes.

"Call me your Master!" Chom demanded.

"My Master!" Gonar cried out, nearly delirious with the ecstasy of freedom from self which his submission brought on.

"Oh, Gonar, you so much wanted a ruby," said Chom, "that I shall give you one!"

He took the gold earring with its dependent scarlet stone from his ear. Gonar saw that it was not a complete ring, but a loop with sharpened points. Chom placed the points at each side of Gonar's right nipple, then took Gonar's cock in his hand and began to stroke it.

Chom's mouth fastened on Gonar's mouth, his tongue invading, probing, raping. Gonar felt his balls struggle to shrink up through the wooden stock: he felt the golden points pierce slowly through his nipple. It was more than the whole rest of his life, and all in a moment.

The golden points rammed through his tit, marking him with Chom's ruby ring. A geyser of semen fought up through his cock and burst in white jets upon his belly, up onto his chest. Chom's mouth and hand pulled away and Chom's huge cock was before him, spurting thick, white gouts upon his face. And Gonar, bound to the chair and owned, at last knew what glory was.

Laura Antoniou

THE WAY OF HEAVEN

The Lady General, Asano Ochina, Mistress of the Four Provinces, Conqueror of the Battle of Kiyoshi, and Special Retainer to the Lord of the Sunlit Isles, bowed her head down to the woven mat and held her position until the barely perceptible movement of her lord's little finger. Although no one else in the room was permitted to keep their arms, her swords glittered from their polished scabbards on her back and in her sash.

"I like this little," Lord Nuri sniffed, leaning delicately toward his companion Lord Kaneto. "This upstart peasant female owns the puissance of a lord twice her age and four times her breeding! The Prince is too much swayed by her."

"Oh, yes, that is surely so," Lord Kaneto flirted back, lowering his eyes demurely.

"And yet, she has served us well upon the fields of battle," interjected young Princess Asa, who was the Great Lord's adopted cousin. The three of them watched as the general's back straightened and she was acknowledged by her lord.

Her armor moved underneath layers of brightly colored woven and knotted silk, bands of crimson and gold overlaid with the crescent-moon-and-clover symbol of the royal house. Her long black hair was bound behind her, and a wide band was wrapped around her forehead, battle style. No other fighter ever dared to enter the court dressed in such an outlandish way. Even the lowest-ranking soldier knew to change into formal kimono and sandals. But not the Lady General.

"Her victories only serve to make her more dangerous," Nuri snarled. "One day, she will rise up and betray the Lord, mark my words."

"You are a fool," whispered the elderly Lord Senji. His bones creaked like armor when he shifted his posture so the younger retainers could hear his carefully modulated words. "You must observe everything, else know nothing. Observe; does she not show him great deference in her every move, in her very choice of inflection and her every breath? Do her eyes never leave his person, ever following the plumes of his breath, her body taut with eagerness to obey? Does not the Great Lord always take his Lady General into private session after her report, in order to hear what is meant only for his ears? And does not the Great Lord always return from such meetings refreshed and full of strength?"

"This is so, Old Lord," the Princess murmured, "but what is it you are suggesting?"

"That the Great Lord is pillowing with his general?" Kaneto muffled a snicker. "Oh, surely not! With a commoner?"

"A further outrage!" Nuri hissed. "She will perhaps try to entice him into a dalliance!"

"You know that is impossible," Lord Senji chided. "Has not the Great Lord already accepted the Lady Echiko to be his wife? No, nothing can come of this, save the continued loyalty and love of his general." He glanced at the two of them conferring at the front of the room, oblivious to the surrounding audience of retainers, guards, and petitioners.

"No, children," the old man sighed, "there is no danger from the general. He has tamed her with his passion, bound her to him through his power. She loves our master and will serve him loyally to death."

Princess Asa nodded and turned her nose away from the gossiping lords, ignoring the slight curl of contempt in Kaneto's lips.

Lord Nuri straightened his own back and composed his handsome face. "She is a viper," he assured Kaneto.

"Oh, she surely is," Kaneto agreed.

"And finally, Lord, here are the agreements of the provincial governing lords, and their written oaths to you. They will arrive in the capital before the first snows to offer their obedience in person, and beg leave to present you with such gifts and tributes as you desire."

Ochina's voice was low and gravelly, the voice of a woman long used to raising sound above the din of a battlefield. Her weathered face framed dark eyes, like pools of still water in moonlight. Even under the exaggerated wings of her formal battle armor, her shoulders looked broad and strong. Her hand, brown and marked by winds, reins, and hilts, and crisscrossed with old scars, extended the rolled sheaf of papers to her lord.

Lord Yoshinake took the scrolls with one clean, smooth, and manicured hand. Although his palms and fingers were also marked by the sword, he had not seen battle from any position closer then scenic overlooks. And why should he? He had been fortunate in finding and obtaining the service of the greatest general in the Isles, and with her strength and his wisdom had nearly succeeded in uniting all of the provinces and kingdoms as they were when the land was new. It was only a matter of time before he would become the first Emperor of the unified Sunlit Isles in centuries.

"We are pleased with our General," he intoned with a grave nod. He was a young man still, barely into his third decade, a child when his father died and left him the swords and fan of the clan. His hair was ink black and swept up onto his head in the style favored by royalty, his cheeks clean, and his skin pale and soft. But he was a serious and calculating lord, full of plans and insights, and he had earned the respect of his retainers.

"We shall now retire into privacy to hear that which is for our ears only," he said, nodding to the room. As one, his court bowed, and his bodyguards sprang up to make way for their lord. He rose while his court was still bowed into rows of colorful backs and smiled briefly at the sight of their heads all bobbing almost to the floor. His general waited to rise herself until her lord was a few steps ahead and followed him at the correct distance.

"A viper!" Nuri repeated.

"As you say," murmured Kaneto, fanning himself.

■ ■ ■

Yoshinake Tetsuo, Lord of the Sunlit Isles, Protector of the Shrines of Kiso, Bearer of the Sacred Regalia, and Prince of the Blood, immediately threw himself down onto his belly when the doors behind him slid shut. He lay there, trembling and quivering like a minnow trapped in a receding tide pool as the sounds of his personal guard echoed away into the distance.

"You are so like a worm," Ochina commented.

"Oh, yes, my lady," he eagerly offered back, not daring to raise his head.

Ochina kicked him once, hard, catching him in the side, near his ribs. "You are forgetful, O Prince."

"My General! My glorious General!"

"Do you know why you are like a worm, O Prince?"

He stiffened and his fists tightened in the effort required to answer her. "I squirm upon the very earth before you, my General?"

Ochina kicked him again, this time catching him in the thigh. "No, you cretin. It is because you are blind, and useful only to catch greater prey. Speaking of which, have you accepted Echiko?"

"Yes, my General!" Eager to be recognized for doing something right, the Prince raised his head, just a little bit. "As you instructed me, my General! She arrives in sixteen days!"

"Good," Ochina murmured. She walked the length of the room, and shrugged her shoulders under the armor. "You may approach me, my royal wormling."

Tetsuo leaped to his feet and tried to contain himself as he crossed the mats to where she stood, rigid and waiting for his ministrations. Carefully, he untied the silk ribbons of her over mantle, and then the straps and ties of her body armor. With the ease of a man who has seen this done thousands of times and learned from the royal valets themselves, he acted the perfect personal servant. With a calm demeanor which did not betray his nervousness, he used his own stand to lay her armor aside, carrying each piece with care and delicacy.

"I remember when you lacked these skills," Ochina chuckled. "I suppose that you do have some use after all."

She turned toward him, the only layer left between them the leather underpadding, soft with use where it was not stiff with repeated washings in sweat and blood. He blushed sweetly, like a girl, and she flicked one finger in his direction. With trembling fingers, Tetsuo untied the knots which held the padding together, and without brushing her skin with his bare hands, drew it off.

Her hard body, brown where the layers of silk and armor failed to cover her and harder and pale where it did, made him moan, a tight sound not quite held in check as he scurried to lay the padding down and return with a light cotton robe. He noted with familiar pangs of sympathetic pain her calluses and her scars, the bruises from her latest engagement, and the white lines that mapped out past ones.

"You are a goddess," he murmured, slipping the cool cotton over her shoulders.

"Wormling," she snorted. "At least you can finally be left on your own. Show me your devotion, O Prince." She seated herself on his mats, pulling one leg up in a vulgar fashion never displayed before such an august presence, and poured herself some of his wine. It had been a waste of time to have him serve it; he never could hear the musical tone of the liquid as it filled the small porcelain cup, and without that understanding, she might as well do it herself. In fact, the casual grace that she displayed in such a simple act shamed him even further. Peasants were not supposed to have such a touch for artistry.

But instead of dwelling on his faults, Tetsuo knelt before her and parted his own robes. His sash was heavy brocade, wound through with precious thread of gold, but he cast it aside without a thought and eagerly parted layers of silk to reveal his artfully folded loincloth. When he unwound it, his tumescent manhood, awakened since the first appearance of his goddess, stirred over the clean, round spheres that housed his future generations. But cast through the head of his royal cock was a device no household servant had seen.

It was a large ring, carved of ivory. It was not a complete circle, but gapped, leaving two points separated by a finger's width. The entire ring could be contained in the circle he made with his thumb and forefinger. On one end of the ring was a knob, carved from the original tusk, and depicting a chrysanthemum bud. The other end of the ring came to a sharp and narrow point. Covering the point now was a golden ball with a pin through it.

The ring actually went into his organ, through the little slit at the end. He remembered himself, bound for his own safety, his mind flooded with entreaties to his ancestors and all the gods (should they exist) that the pain would be endurable and that he would show no discomfort. He did his ancestors proud in that respect, although he privately doubted that many of them approved of the nature of the pain he endured. But that was not his fault; these were different times. It was no longer the custom of a prince to actually do battle in the field. He must have his mettle tested in more esoteric endeavors.

Ochina had affixed this ornament herself, hammering the gold around the point with the edge of her chop. Tetsuo could have easily removed the appliance had he wished, but he could have never duplicated her own design in the soft gold if he marred it in any way.

The Lady General gazed at the displayed royal genitalia and nodded. "You have been good, my princeling," she said generously. "And you are still as pretty as a girl."

He beamed with pleasure, another thing his court never saw. "Thank you, my General!"

"Come closer," she commanded.

Eagerly, he shuffled forward, and displayed his pretty body for her pleasure. His bare chest shone with scented oils; his body was clean of the few hairs that grew when he did not order his barber to remove them. He was strong and healthy and in his prime, and the sedentary life at court did not prevent him from engaging in regular exercise with swords and bows, or long rides through the countryside, hunting and taking the air. His nipples seemed somewhat larger then those of other men, but that was also because of his goddess. Even now, she reached for them first, testing them with tight pinching and a light slap of her rough fingertips. Tetsuo sighed with pleasure.

"These shall have to be schooled again," she said softly. "They are unused to attention. I have brought with me wooden pegs which we shall employ later. Eventually, I shall have made matching rings, so that you may be decorated here as well."

Tetsuo opened his eyes and bit the inside of his lip. "My General ... nothing would please me more ... yet ... my

General surely knows ... it will be very difficult for me to hide such rings! I will have to dismiss my dressers entirely, and forbid all from my bath, and never strip to the waist during competition!"

Ochina nodded, a slight smile on her lips. "Yes, that is true," she acknowledged. Her eyes flashed across his body appreciably. "But by that time, you will have already firmly established your ... eccentricities. Your court will believe this to be some new fad of yours, and you will create fashion. It is already said in Jito-Myo that the most civilized of men will never bare their generative organs to less-than-equals." She smiled again and moved her fingers down to stroke the length of his shaft, which swelled at her touch. It was also clean and sweet smelling, the skin as smooth as heavy silk. She stroked it absently, like a pet, until it rose and jutted out, and Tetsuo sucked in a quick breath to prepare for the usual response to such behavior.

Her hand swept away from the royal cock and then back with a sharp slap, so that it swung to one side, struck his upper thigh, and rebounded back. Tetsuo ground his teeth, but stayed still, his muscles tense. She slapped him again for good measure, and he arched his back, appeasing her by offering her yet more.

"My princeling," she chuckled warmly. She returned to sipping at the wine, watching him recover, his flesh pulsating with power and desire, and his body betraying nothing of the minor pain she had caused him.

Together, they breathed in the rich scent of power. When it began to dissipate, Ochina sighed and shook her head. "Unbraid my hair," she said, pouring more of the wine. Tetsuo crawled behind her and began to undo the practical windings of her hair with gentle and skilled fingers.

"My General," he ventured, as he reached for the second braid, "your miserable servant has ... a concern."

"Yes?" There was just an edge of impatience in her voice.

"The Lady Echiko..." He faltered, despite having practiced a myriad of methods for approaching this delicate subject. "She is to be my wife..."

Ochina chuckled again. "Yes, my worm-prince, she shall. And therefore, we will have to remove your special ring so that you may present her with your royal bratlings. But it will return as soon as your princely duties are done."

Tetsuo sighed and brightened immediately. "Then ... you shall meet me before and after each visit to the lady?"

"At first. Until Echiko learns herself how to remove and apply it."

Tetsuo's fingers fumbled and he drew them out of her hair in panic. "My General?"

"Finish what you are doing, you fool. That will cost you many stripes later." As his trembling fingers returned to working out the weaving of her tresses, she smiled, knowing that he couldn't see her face. How delightful it was to surprise him! Even the wise Prince could not possibly guess all of the twists and mysteries of her imagination. She hardened her voice, for her pleasure and his. "Were you so foolish to think that after capturing your manhood myself I would allow you to exercise it elsewhere? No, my prince, you are mine, from the moment I first held you down and opened you, to the day you leave this world and go to meet your ancestors."

"B-but ... Echiko!"

"She will learn to keep you," Ochina stated. "I shall teach her myself. Echiko and I have ... met before." She coughed out a laugh, a low sound like the growling of a caged hunting cat, and she could actually feel the trembling of Tetsuo's fingers as he realized the whole of this new chapter in his tale.

"I am sure she will be amenable to your situation," Ochina continued. "In sixteen days, when she arrives, you will send her at once to me, and I shall teach her how to properly train you, use you, and keep you obedient and pleasing."

"But what shall I tell my court? That is most irregular!" Tetsuo's panic had grown considerably.

"Bear yourself like a man, you excrement of turtles," Ochina snapped. "You will tell your royal bottom-kissers that the lady requires training in arms, as a good warlord's wife should have and that since you have the greatest female fighter in the world at your service, you shall use her to instruct your wife. Ten days from her arrival, you will set the date for your marriage ... I have decided that the fifth day of the Month of the Falling Blossoms will be auspicious for the wedding."

Tetsuo's mouth fell open in amazement, and he buried his attention to his task, running his shaking fingers through her hair until it shone in waves of shimmering ink. Oddly, his mind fastened upon the word *auspicious,* and he wondered if his general had actually consulted the appropriate astrologers. Then, he remembered the astonishing revelation about his future bride, and scampered on his knees back in front of her, where he bowed deeply.

"Most honored General," he whispered, his forehead touching the surface of the mat. He held the position, his back muscles tense with the strain of the formal posture. "Your worthless slave begs for your attention!"

The Lady General gazed down on the bow that his back made. It was strong, bent like a cedar limb under great weight, an expanse of wheat blown over by a southern wind. She could see the faint lines she had once drawn with bamboo rods, broken across that expanse, tearing flesh and marking him the way everything she did marked him forever. Ah, but that had been magnificent! To indulge their drives so strongly that blood flew between them and the very earth rumbled with pleasure in their frenzy. But it had been some time since they had such freedom.

"You need to be taken," she said finally, her voice strangely soft. "You need to be held, like a girl child before pillowing, an old man before dying. It is not seeming that I, a descendant of peasants, be your lady, so there must be another. And Echiko is suitable. She is amenable. And you will show her all the honor the wife of an Emperor deserves and she will be your taker, and your keeper."

The Lord of the Sunlit Isles shook as he raised his head to gaze at his beloved general. His lovely eyes were bright with devotion, but his face was composed, his lips parted only slightly. "This crawling one is overwhelmed by his General's forethought and generosity," he whispered. "But he fears for the loss of his one true master. He begs that the General reconsider. Please do not leave this broken one to the hands of a child!"

"You know the tones very well, my princeling," Ochina admitted, leaning forward. "And you flatter me with them. But do not fear; Echiko may be a child, but she is no novice to the use of a man such as you. Did you believe that I would cast you into the care of an incompetent? That I would abandon my ruler to the whims of a mere girl? Oh no, my prince. Echiko and I have already planned what shall become of you. And there are many more years in these scarred limbs of mine, many more battles to your honor and power and glory before the gods (if they exist). Before I go to face my ancestors, I will be assured that you will be astride the Dragon Throne and surrounded by little grubs of royal birth to carry the swords when you have returned to me in the Other Kingdoms."

Tetsuo bowed his head again in mute acceptance, and shivered as she drew her fingers along his jaw.

"My princeling," she murmured, patting his cheek and smoothing her hand over his warrior's knot. "I will serve you unto death and beyond. Come to me, my worm, my dog, my soon-to-be Emperor, and please me. Perhaps if you do, I shall permit you to achieve clouds and rain tomorrow, or the day after. And perhaps I will not." She sighed and leaned back and parted the light robe she wore. "Come to me, my great lord."

And like the princely worm he was, Tetsuo crawled forward, to the divided thighs of the Lady General, Asano Ochina, Mistress of the Four Provinces, Conqueror of the Battle of Kiyoshi, and Special Retainer to him.

TRUTH OR DARE?

"**S**o you want to be a boy."

My master loomed over me as I knelt, head bowed to the proper angle, in front of him. The white sun of Nova Vegas sent a sharp shadow of his head over me as he looked me up and down, slowly, as if he didn't like what he saw.

"Is this because you know that I really wanted a boy slave, and only selected you because you were far and away the best of that sorry lot Kamal had for sale?"

"No, Master."

"Have you been talking with my former slaves? Marco, perhaps, or Achilles? Did they talk about how I treated them and make you dissatisfied with your present lot?"

"No, Master. I have spoken with no one about you."

He narrowed his dark brown eyes. "Is it that you want to be more like me? Is that your secret thought?"

"No, Master."

"Then why?"

I shifted in my kneeling position to ease the pressure both on my knees and in my heart, unable to answer in ritual phrases.

He took my chin in his hand and tilted it up to read my face. "Why, Drusilla?" he repeated, and I knew he wanted my best, most honest answer. He never forces me to raise my eyes unless he wants the absolute truth.

I just wished I knew what to tell him. What was the truth?

"I—with you, I am a boy, Master. In all the ways but the expression of gender, compared to you, in relation to you, with you, I am a boy. Young, and fumbling, and eager, and scared. I just want to be truer to that, Master. Truer to how I feel."

He sighed. "You've only been here a few weeks. Can you be that sure? It's not some glamour that surrounds me in your eyes that will fade with time? A phase that you will grow out of? In five years, when you are free, you may feel differently."

I tried to drop my eyes again, but his fingers gripped my jaw as if he would crush it any moment and his eyes probed me. I did not flinch. "I am your boy, Master. I am."

With a nod of finality he let me drop my head, and sighed again. "All right, Drusilla. If this is just a passing fancy, the three months of training I'll put you through will knock you back into reality. You may quit at any time. But if you quit, I never wish to hear of this again, understand? I bought you because I liked your boldness, but even so there are limits to what I will accept in a slave. Do not make me regret my choice."

I kissed his boots fervently, the cuffs of his silk suit slick against my face. "I promise, Master. Thank you, Master."

■ ■ ■

Three months. Three months of running and jumping and crawling and climbing. Three months of having my head shaved and my face rubbed in the sand as I wrestled with the other boys on the estate. Three months of hell that I hoped would lead to my own personal heaven.

All the advertisements had said, "On Nova Vegas, the gambling island, life itself is just a game." I had come and, spellbound by the glitter and the excitement, gambled my life itself away. Now I was learning just how intricate the games, the players, and the rules of Nova Vegas could be.

I had been an indoor pet; now I did all the outdoor chores. I chopped logs for the huge fireplace, cleaned the chimney, got grubby under the hoods and chassis of the master's cars and limos. If there was gardening, chauffeuring or just heavy loading to be done, I was the one they called. There were times I was close to despair, but the tasks never broke me, just pushed me a little further with each passing day.

At night the butler brought me into the house and had me dress and undress in clothes that I had seen only from the outside. Now I was in them, learning the mystery of opposite-buttoning shirts, fancy-dress pants with the extra interior button across, and boxer shorts that rode up on me until I felt as if I balanced on a hot razor, as well as the lace-up work boots and overalls that were my customary lot.

My crotch ached where the material confined or rubbed it, and every night as I lay on my bed of straw in the stables—a far cry from my silken pallet inside!—I grasped the mons as if pulling on an imaginary cock. But the sensation was not strong enough yet and I ended up more frustrated than ever.

The butler made me practice walking and standing until my legs hurt. "Stride, boy, stride. Don't mince your steps like a girl. These are men's shoes you're trying to fill." When I complained or was otherwise unsatisfactory, he called the housekeeper in and she caned me like a naughty schoolboy, past the point where I yelped and screamed for mercy.

During those sessions, the butler allowed me to cry, but issued the warning, "Even when you cry, you have to cry like a man. Swallow hard. That's it. Swallow again, as you try to hold the tears back and they come anyway because it hurts—" and another swing of the cane would punctuate that.

Opening doors, lighting cigarettes, bowing and kissing hands, keeping my voice as low as possible. At nineteen, most men knew these rituals by heart. I had three months. Would I pass? Could I make it true?

And always my master's eyes were on me, gauging me. He never smiled, and never spoke directly to me. It was "get the boy to do it" or "send for the boy." But on occasion he would cuff me on the head wordlessly, a sign of rough affection which I treasured. It meant he was pleased and I was succeeding.

And I shined all his boots, which all smelled of leather and dirt and him, and happily swallowed my tears.

■ ■ ■ ■

Three months. Ninety days. On the ninety-first day, I awoke on my pallet in the stables to find the chauffeur standing over me.

"Come on, boy. It's examination day. You're to meet the master at a fancy society party this afternoon and see if you can pass the final test."

He grinned as he led me into the house, but would not tell me any more no matter how I begged him. On my former bedding were laid out a tuxedo and ruffled dress shirt, along with a pair of wingtip shoes with correct black socks and a pair of plain white briefs. Next to that had been placed a wallet with some money in it, a cigarette case and lighter, and an engraved invitation addressed to "Drew Grant."

I looked suspiciously at the chauffeur. "There ought to be a handkerchief here as well."

He laughed, showing white teeth against his small Italian face. "Here," he said, producing a folded square of undecorated cotton from his jacket, "just come out to the car when you're done."

As he left, I blinked as I realized that I had just passed the first test.

■■■■

I entered the anteroom, where a servant accepted the invitation; after scrutinizing its every detail, he accepted it, and me, as genuine. "May I take your coat, sir, and say how glad we are to have you here?"

He plucked the topcoat from my shoulders with the ease of long practice. "Is my patron, Mr. Smythe, here yet?" I asked, trying not so sound as nervous as I felt. I would feel better with my master's presence to lend me assurance.

He spread his hands in dismay. "Alas, Mr. Smythe came by earlier to ask me to tell you that he will be delayed by an unexpected appointment, but that you should amuse yourself until he arrives."

He started to turn away, and I squared my shoulders and set my jaw. So I was on my own. My nerves twitched and I wanted to run. But I wasn't just proving myself to my master; I was proving myself to myself. And so this was something I would have to do by myself exactly as I would have in his presence.

There was the mandatory copy of *Debee's English Peerage and Propriety* on the entryway table; I touched the elaborate leather binding for good luck. The original colonists of Nova Vegas had been fifty-five nobles and their retinues, returning from their holdings in the New World to attend the Virgin Queen's wedding ... only to be shipwrecked, with a single tattered copy of *Debee's* the sole reminder of their former life. They had then clung to that elaborate social structure with all the tenacious insanity of the hopelessly marooned.

Rediscovered two hundred years later by one of Gutenberg's early steamships, the tropical island was now a resort for the postwar wealthy, who were enchanted by the exotic setting and story. And besides, who could resist a chance to join in the longest-running masquerade in history?

But like any witch worth her salt, Nova Vegas could not resist playing the occasional nasty trick on its visitors...

Like stripping me of all that I was, and then giving me to a master who changed my life with a single look.

I straightened my tie in the mirror and started to go in. A hand caught my elbow, and the manservant gave a polite cough.

"Yes?"

The manservant dropped his eyes. "Please understand that Mr. Smythe left explicit instructions with me that I should not give this to you unless you did not ask for any further explanation of his absence." A small envelope, the size of a calling card, dropped into my hand. "That was his express wish, and I have found that it is best to obey him to the letter."

His eyes were knowing. I bowed my head slightly. "Of course. I understand perfectly. I will assure him that you fulfilled your duties to the letter."

He gave a quarter-of-an-inch nod, his face expressionless except for a tell-tale gleam in his eye that announced he had some knowledge on his part of the true state of affairs between my master and myself. His voice was so soft I almost missed it. "As will I," he murmured, turning to greet the next party that had stepped laughingly through the door.

■ ■ ■ ■

I opened the envelope and withdrew a card. On the front, printed in uncompromising Cochin Bold, it read: Master Regis Smythe. On the verso, penned in my master's broad hand, it read:

Drew, present this card to my close friend Miss Daniela Stratford, with my compliments.

A slip of light aqua paper showed itself as I began to return the card neatly to the envelope. That paper added the kicker:

You may wish to add your own as well; if you are so inclined, you are instructed to do so to the fullest of your ability.

After reading it several times, I began to shake at what underlay those casual, polite words. My final test was clear: to deal with Miss Stratford in my character as "Drew," not only to engage her in such a way that my masculinity would be established without question, but perhaps even to respond to her femininity as a normal man would.

Just how far did he expect me to go with this response?

I reviewed the design of all my training, leading up to this point, and decided I must go as far as I could, for my master had always required that of me, and would judge me on that basis.

■■■■

Inside, some mad post-WWIV decorator had tried to cross a Venetian palace with an Edwardian smoking-room, and nearly succeeded. But the mixed marriage of light and dark luxury dissolved under the massed impact of dozens of men in their dark, clean lines and dozens of women in their puffy party dresses.

It had been so long since I moved in society without being a slave, I had to suppress my impulse to drop my gaze only to their feet. I forced polite smiles at those who nodded to me. My head was ordering my legs to move slowly and confidently across the floor, while my heart was thumping in my rib cage.

Dresses of emerald, ruby, and sapphire floated adrift in the sea of pearl walls, tiger's-eye paneling, and obsidian floor. I smiled at each woman I passed, deliberately enough to be friendly but quickly enough not to be misinterpreted.

Where was the hostess? It would be impolite to walk up to a woman and introduce myself. Or was that another part of my assignment, to see how forward I could push in my new role?

Thank goodness, the hostess found me. Mrs. Abercrombie spotted me looking lost and, like any fine hostess, excused herself with swift grace from a conversation to come to my rescue—a stout middle-aged dowager setting determined sail for me through the wash of crowd. Darting over with the easy gait of a woman born to horses, she put out a warm hand which I bowed over and kissed with all my hard-won delicacy.

"You must be Mr. Smythe's new boy, Drew. I would have known you anywhere from his description. Born to wear a suit, he said you were, and I must say you do look quite fine in it. I only wish my husband wore his tuxedo with such style." She waved her other hand at her colonel-husband, stiff and uncomfortable beside the fireplace as he barked at other middle-aged men.

She made sure I had a drink and introduced me to some of the partygoers, then moved off once she had me established in a crowd of young men. Her son, Taylor, took me under his wing then, when it turned out we had a shared passion for antique Triumph and MG sports cars.

He leaned familiarly on my shoulder as we talked, and as he breathed confidences to me I could tell he'd gassed himself quite full to survive the party. I envied him; I was afraid that if I drank too much I might slip in character and fail my test, so I took very small sips of my scotch-and-soda.

"Take the TR-3!" he exclaimed, swaying like the floor had become a deck cleaving through swells that prophesied a coming storm. "Gorgeous but temperamental. Like Daniela over there," nodding his head in the direction of the bay windows, "wouldn't you say, Drew?"

I shook my head no, suppressing the shake in the rest of my body at the mention of the uncommon name of Daniela. "I haven't had the pleasure of meeting the woman, Taylor, so I don't know if that comparison is true or not."

"Back me up here, Nigel. Don't I have the divine Daniela pegged? Gorgeous but temperamental."

Nigel rolled his pale eyes as he lounged across an armchair, swinging his leg. "Oh, absolutely, Taylor. Sweet as sugar one moment, but if you disappoint her, she's got a devastating tongue."

Taylor winced. "Don't I know it! I shouldn't have drunk so much that night, and she doesn't give second chances. But you say you haven't met her, Drew? I'll introduce you, then. And then you tell me what you make of her."

I followed him across the room to a collection of chairs and sofas next to the bay window. Several of the young women had withdrawn here and were discussing something that had them giggling as Taylor approached. When they became aware of him, a soft mezzo-soprano said something inaudible, and the giggling redoubled.

Taylor frowned, but the liquor had insulated his ego, and besides, he wasn't going to let them annoy him. "My friend Drew here says he hasn't met you yet, Daniela. Knowing you, I find that hard to believe, but he didn't recognize you by my description."

The same voice that had made the earlier comment now made itself plain. "How thoughtful of you to remedy that, Taylor dear. Bring him forward, please, if you're going to present him to me."

Another, shriller voice snapped off to my left, "Or is that make a present of him to you? Like a cat laying a slain mouse at one's feet. Or a bird dog bringing back wounded prey?"

Daniela shot back, "May I kindly suggest that you shut up, Mary, until you have something worth saying? Taylor may be many things, some of them not as pleasant as others perhaps, but he is a decent and honorable man and I will not stand for his being referred to, however indirectly, as a genteel version of a pimp. He is not to be injured in that fashion."

Her words sallied forth in such breathtaking speed and array that I was still trying to work out if she had complimented or insulted Taylor when he grabbed my elbow and shoved me forward with an exasperated mutter of "See what I mean?"

"Daniela Stratford, may I present Drew Grant." Taylor pushed me a little farther forward, and then we were facing each other.

Young, and fumbling, and eager, and scared. Oh, she made me feel all of that. In contrast to the other women, wafting in clouds of colored taffeta and satin, she was direct and forward in a slender gown of green-and-gold diamond-patterned silk held over her broad shoulders by thin chains of gold. Her pageboy of black hair slid over her tan shoulders.

The other women used the fluffy aspects of their gowns to disguise bumps and bulges; her silk dress hid nothing and was all the sexier for it. The other women were still pretending that they were girls. She was a woman and unashamed of the fact.

"Nice to meet you, Mr. Grant." I kissed her hand, sweet with the scent of violets, in greeting.

She tilted her head at Taylor as I straightened. "I see what you mean, Taylor. I find it hard to believe that we haven't met before as well. His manners are nearly as good as yours."

Taylor had a purple bewildered look on his face. A good ten years her junior, he was way out of his depth with her. For that matter, so was I. But this was the task set for me, so I had to try my best.

I didn't want to make an enemy of Taylor, and so I flashed him my best roguish smile and said, "I see what you mean as well, Taylor. She is definitely both."

That mollified him, but a wave of uncomfortable laughter rippled through the group; what did I mean by "both"?

The others were afraid to ask. A corner of Daniela's lip lifted and she turned her gaze full to me. "Both what, Mr. Grant?"

She could have directed that question at Taylor and royally skewered him, but it wouldn't have been fair and she and I both knew it. Taylor escaped under cover of my bow to her and my honest response. "You were described to me as resembling the classic TR-3 sports car."

The laughter came a little louder behind my back. This was a risky tactic, and if it failed I was doomed. But I thought I had judged her strength well enough to try it.

"Really?" she said, her face motionless. "And that resemblance is?"

I left the comment in its original form, rather than reversing it to take out some of the sting. I had to match the precise sharpness of her wit, or come across as an utter fool. "That you are gorgeous, but temperamental."

Daniela let me hang out on my limb for agonizing moments where my feet turned cold and my palms sweated. As the obvious leader in this group, her reaction would mark me as clever or a boor. Had I won or lost?

In that moment I saw her: the Gypsy Queen of Gamblers, her graceful lacquered hand poised to pluck a card from the deck and her keen dark aqua eyes about to glance at the image that would reveal my fate. Oh, I knew her caprices well, that personification of Lady Luck that blazed from the placards and shimmered in the commercial holographia. I had cursed her roundly when I lost my fortune at the table and was sold into slavery, but now I knew better. What I had seen as bad luck had simply been another move in the game for her, a raising of the stakes. My master was all the fortune I could ever desire.

So once again I gambled everything on one throw, for the life I sought to have with my new master, and hoped she would smile on my daring, rather than slap me for my impudence.

"I appreciate the breathtaking freshness of youth," she said, and smiled.

Everyone breathed.

The group turned to each other to make the chatter of the mindless and release the tension of the encounter, so they missed the terrifying spectacle of that sweet smile broadening into the welcoming smile of a man-eating tiger.

"You're going to be mine, boy," it promised.

I could feel myself swelling, almost as if I had a cock and could respond as expected to her invitation. I met her gaze with my best look of challenge. "And you mine," my bold eyes promised as well. I didn't know how yet, but I would make it as true as I had everything else.

The look in her eyes retreated as she introduced me to the others around the circle.

"Mary" turned out to have a pretty face but a sulky lower lip. Sophie, Julie, Megan, Ursula, Betty, Theresa all batted their eyes as I kissed their hands, floating through my vision like a school of fish looking for a kind shark to devour them. I began to understand the pride of the peacock male as they responded in some way to my bearing and my words, my light flirtations and my light rebuffs. So I paraded my maleness, not as a naked cock but as an unmistakable attitude and ability.

Not once did I break character to look at Daniela, but I could feel her eyes on me, assessing me. Finally I felt I had shown off enough that the presentation of my master's card to her would be a graceful addition and not an obvious act to curry favor. I knelt to the level of her seat and gave her the card.

"My patron, Mr. Smythe, asked to be remembered to you, Miss Stratford, with his compliments. Apparently he was detained elsewhere, but he promised to be here at some point."

Daniela raised an eyebrow as she smiled. "Ah, now I know where you got those beautiful manners, Mr. Grant. Regis"—her dark voice slurred it the Porto-French way, as Re-zhie, rather than the Jap-Chop Ree-jis—"would expect no less of you."

"Have you known him long?" Her casual reference to my master made me ache all the worse, torn between my new longing to enjoy her luscious body at luxurious length, and my guilty remembrance of how a gentle slap from my master's hand on my butt had always been enough to make me come like a rocket.

Daniela rolled her eyes. "Ages, it seems. And you?"

"Only a few months. But he's taught me a great deal."

Testing the waters again. How well did she know Mr. Smythe?

"Oh, I'm sure he has," she replied, and what her flat statement did not say her quick glance did. The suggestion underlying her comment burned me inside. I wasn't sure how long I could stand her teasing. How much did she know?

"And now he's introducing you into society to further your education," she continued, tucking the card unself-consciously into her cleavage. "Honestly, Regis thinks of everything."

I imagined the writing of the card rubbing off on her breast as she moved and twisted and sweated under my tongue and hands...

I jerked back to attention, sternly reminding myself not to get out of hand here, and searched for a suitable reply to her comment. "I'm indebted to him, in a sense."

If she knew my true status as his slave, her face didn't betray it in the slightest. "Why is that?"

"Well, for one thing, because his suggestion to attend this party allowed me to meet you, Miss Stratford."

The dark eyebrow raised again. "You have very nice manners indeed, Mr. Grant." She leaned forward from her slouch slightly. "Do you ever drop them?" she said in the same nonchalant voice.

I dropped the volume of my voice, clenching the bottom muscles of my throat hard to keep my voice low as well. "As the lady, it is for you to say. I kneel at your feet; I am at your command. If you want me to, I will."

"Touche," she said, speaking little short of a whisper. "Yes, Drew, I do want you to."

The way she strung out that phrase, I could almost feel the tug of an invisible leash. "Whatever pleases you ... Daniela."

A shout came from Taylor, running from the windows.

"Fire! Fire! Father, the barns are on fire!"

The colonel, jerked awake from his boring conversation, seemed relieved by a chance for quick and decisive action and was already rounding up the servants and dispatching them with swift orders.

The party, curious, jammed the windows to watch the fun.

Daniela stood, straightened her dress, but made no move to join the others. No one was watching us now.

That heated smile returned to her face as she looked down at my kneeling form as if contemplating a particularly juicy piece of prey.

"Truth or Dare?" she taunted.

"Dare," I said as I rose and grabbed her hand and we fled into the deserted hallway. Her touch was scorching me, her hand was hot and dry and I felt as if we would both go up in flames to echo the burning barns if we had to wait a moment longer.

"Where?"

"To the left," she pointed to a low paneled hallway. "I'm staying in a guest room."

It was a small room, taken up mostly by an overstuffed armchair, a marble-topped dresser carved with cupids, and a huge feather bed. I pulled her to me, kissing her lips that shone a dark glossy rose under the low light of the candle-lamps on the walls. She smelled of damp violets, and the earth they grew from, and I buried my face in her hair, nuzzling and tasting her skin as my hands sought for a way into her dress.

The silk slid and stretched but refused to part. The strain in her body beneath the fabric drove me mad; we were both desperate for release, and I couldn't give it to her yet. When I was a woman, I knew how dresses like this worked—

When I was a woman. The reminder stopped me cold. All along, I had been acting as if I really could be a man for Daniela, and now reality was a cold slap in my burning face. How in the world was I going to give her the release she craved?

I drew back, my heart sinking. I knew Daniela would make me pay dearly for this, for arousing her to this pitch and then not following through. And I was going to fail my master's test, in the most embarrassing way possible.

Daniela's eyes bit into me. "What's wrong, Drew? Don't you want me?"

I raised my hands in a mute gesture of appeal. "I do, Daniela, you don't know how much! I want you, but I can't..." I grabbed her hand and held it directly to my crotch. I was hot, I was soaked, I was swollen, but my biology still didn't correspond to what I had in my head.

She grabbed me by the ears and tried to look into my face. "Are you a boy or a girl?"

I was too humiliated to look at her. "Daniela..."

She slapped me then to get my attention. "Answer me, Drew. Are you a boy, or a girl?"

My ugly confession started, and then something side-tracked it. "I'm—I'm a boy, only..."

Her face was in too much shadow to read, but I almost thought I saw a look of satisfaction cross it. "You're absolutely right, Drew, you are a boy. My boy. In every way that counts."

She reached into the dresser and pulled out a harness with a vaginal plug for me and a latex dildo sticking out of the front. "Let's both slip into something more comfortable here. You put this on and I'll struggle out of this gown somehow."

I pulled on the harness. The plug closed my cunt and gave it the solid feeling of the male body, and the actual weight of the cock settled into exactly the place my psychology had placed it.

The need to fuck was so urgent that the rip of a zipper got my immediate attention. Daniela stood naked in the yellow light, brown nipples and black muff shadows against her golden body. I could see now how the silk had smoothed out the naked strength of her body.

She raised her arms and smiled, all teeth. "Come here, boy."

I shoved her down on the bed and she spread her legs for me, her cunt dampened and darkened so with her own need that it looked as if she had applied creamy rouge to it from a pot. My cock stiffened until I thought it would burst, I would burst.

I jumped onto the bed after her and raised my hips between her legs. She moaned as I covered her mouth with mine and pushed into her, feeling inch after soft inch part before me. Heat. I prickled with it, flowed with it, it drove me into her again and again. She was screaming my name, I was screaming something I can't even remember, and then she rolled under me in waves as her orgasm took her and I took her with teasing strokes that built the crests rather than disturbed them.

Her body clenched and then relaxed as we sank further into the bed than seemed realistically possible. As she stopped making sounds, the palm of her flat hand delivered a solid swat to my ass.

Just one, but one was all it had ever taken.

Dark lilac spread throughout my brain as the muscles jerked and let go. I cried out unthinkingly, "Master! Master!

Please, Master!" as the memories behind that single gesture and my long-delayed release left me drained of energy, though not desire ... or, for that matter, of guilt.

If this had been my final test, in one way I had passed but in another I had failed worse than I had even dreamed possible. I felt as if I had betrayed my Master, gone much too far with Daniela. She would doubtless report to him all that I had said and done, including my betrayal, and he would sell me away for being so ungrateful and disobedient. After all he had done for me, how could I have done it?

I swallowed hard. The tears were close, but I could not let them out. Even now, I had to be true to myself. I was a lost boy, but I was now and forever a boy.

Daniela smiled up at me, her face relaxed and happy.

"You're a good boy, Drew."

I jumped back from lying on top of her, because she spoke with the voice of my Master. That growl—

Her left hand plucked an aqua contact from one brown eye, and her right hand pulled the black wig off of her short chestnut hair. My chest bore streaks of the tan makeup she had covered her body with. She sat up and cupped my chin in her hand, the cemented-on nails pressing into my jaw and allowing me, suddenly, an excuse to cry.

"Who are you, Drew?"

"I'm your boy," I sobbed.

"And who am I?"

"You're my Master."

She reached under the pillow to pull out a harness similar to the one I wore and strapped it on herself with the ease of long practice. "Right on both counts," she confirmed as she pushed my chest down the bed.

I prepared, as a boy, to receive my Master's cock.

ABOUT THE CONTRIBUTORS

Laura Antoniou is a kinky, queer native New Yorker who is compulsively involved in publishing. In the past three years, she's edited six anthologies, including the lesbian bestsellers *Leatherwomen* I and II, and *Looking for Mr. Preston,* a fundraising memorial anthology honoring the late John Preston. Under the name Sara Adamson, she is the author of the Marketplace series of erotic novels. She is currently working on several more anthologies, and at least one or two other projects. One day, she hopes to prove that she can actually make a living doing this.

Gary Bowen is the author of the novel *Diary of a Vampire* (Masquerade Books, 1995), and his short fiction has appeared in magazines and anthologies far too numerous to list. A collection of his erotic science fiction short stories, *Queer Destinies,* was published by Circlet Press in 1994, and a collection of erotic fiction, *Man Hungry,* is forthcoming from BadBoy Books in 1996. Obelesk Books published *Winter of the Soul,* a collection of his gay vampire fiction, in 1995. His next project is editing *Western Trails,* a collection of erotic gay western stories for Masquerade Books.

Erik Buck is a bearded, dirty old man who is a prolific writer of erotica and science fiction. Formerly, he was a research physicist and, before that, an Air Force officer. This is his first appearance in a Circlet Press collection.

Reina Delacroix is the pen name of a shy, quiet librarian who lives in northern Virginia with her cats, George and Shen T'ien, and her precious Pet, Michael, and her loyal Wolf, Marc. Her work appears in the Circlet Press anthologies *Feline Fetishes, SexMagick,* and *The Beast Within.*

Raven Kaldera is a pansexual leather pagan whose S/M short stories appear in several Circlet Press anthologies, including *S/M Futures* and *Blood Kiss.*

Jim Lee has published a variety of work in a bewildering assortment of markets since 1982, beginning with an erotic sf poem in Millea Kenin's *Aliens and Lovers* anthology. Recent publications include fiction in *Aberrations, Hardboiled, Fantastic Collectibles, Hustler Fantasies, Bizarre Sex* 3 (Tal Publications), and the anthology *Selling Venus* (Circlet Press, 1995). The 1915 uprising in Malawi (as Nyasaland is known today) proved that, even during the greater slaughter of WWI, white colonials feared black nationalism more than they did one another.

Laurie O is a writer living and working on the northern California coast, near an on-ramp to the information superhighway. She is an enthusiastic participant in the Bay Area's Living History, Celtic Dance, and Science Fiction communities by day, and an e-mail junkie and leather girl by night.

Mason Powell was born on a cable car. His mother was a professional woman—his father was the Pacific fleet. He has appeared as a serious actor in some of the worst porn movies ever made. He is the author of four published novels, one published work of nonfiction, and some forty published short stories in places such as *Mach, Manifest Reader,* and *Drummer,* as well as numerous science fiction stories in the U.S. and abroad. His most famous work is *The Brig.*

Lee Seed, the cover artist, has produced many fine, award-winning illustrations for science fiction/fantasy magazines and science fiction art shows. Her work also graces the covers of Circlet Press's *Selling Venus* and *Virtual Girls.* Commissions are welcome.

Alan Smale settled in the U.S. seven years ago, following an English childhood and an Oxford education. Alan sings bass in two a cappella groups and acts in community theatre, and has made short fiction sales to *A Wizard's Dozen, Marion Zimmer Bradley's Fantasy Magazine, Argonaut,* and *Terminal Fright;* a few more would be nice, to pave the way for the novel that's coming together rather slowly. Ah, if only that day job didn't keep getting in the way...

Cecilia Tan is the publisher and founder of Circlet Press, for which she has edited over a dozen anthologies of erotic science fiction and fantasy. She is the author of *Telepaths Don't Need*

Safewords (Circlet Press, 1992) and her erotic short stories have appeared in numerous places from *Penthouse* to *Ms.* magazine. (If you *really* want a complete list, check out the Web page at http://apocalypse.org/pub/u/ctan/home.html or send an SASE c/o Circlet Press.) Her S/M science fiction novel, *The Velderet,* is being serialized in *Taste of Latex* magazine.

Born in northern British Columbia, **Lynda J. Williams** holds two postgraduate degrees, in information and computer science. Married for eleven years, she has three children, the youngest born late in 1994. She has worked in journalism, librarianship, technical support, and teaches and publishes articles about the Internet. Science fiction has been a passion for her since childhood and she is writing novels featuring the world of "The Bride's Story."